For Betty,
Whose glorious music first inspired me to write about a musician –
With love + admiration
Lila

Strike a Golden Chord

Other Books by Lila Hopkins

Weave Me A Song

Young Adult Fiction

Talking Turkey
Eating Crow

Nonfiction

Victors In The Land

Strike a Golden Chord

by

Lila Hopkins

A novel: A story of unselfishness and sacrifice,
suspense and horror,
revealing what really counts in love:
trust and faith

High Country Publishers, Ltd

Boone, North Carolina
2003

Published in the United States by:
High Country Publishers, Ltd
197 New Market Center #135
Boone, NC 28607
(828) 964-0590
Fax: (828) 262-1973
www.highcountrypublishers.com

Library of Congress Cataloging-in-Publication Data

Hopkins, Lila.
Strike a golden chord / by Lila Hopkins.— 1st ed.
p. cm.
ISBN 1-932158-51-0 (hardcover : alk. paper)
1. Booksellers and bookselling—Fiction. 2. Women booksellers—Fiction.
3. Self-sacrifice—Fiction. 4. North Carolina—Fiction. I. Title.
PS3558.O063546S77 2003
813'.54—dc21

2003008441

Manufactured in the United States of America
First edition: October 2003

Acknowledgments

As always, thanks to my writing pals in High Country Writers, Boone, North Carolina, who take the time to critique and encourage me.

Carolyn Howser proofread the manuscript to the letter, and I thank her for her sharp eyes and meticulous work.

I thank my musician friends, who occasionally let me pretend I am one of them. Betty Watson, Ruth Sinclair, Linda Bell: all church organists who inspire the angels.

To Dr. Lenore McCroskey, Professor of Organ and Harpsichord at North Texas University in Denton, Texas: Your helpful suggestions and encouragement made writing this book possible. Thank you for calling it a "fun" book. I wish I could write the way you play.

Christy Hopkins, my first grandchild, gave me some advice on makeup and hair styles for Joanna and Beth.

The success of a book depends a lot on the working relationship between author and editor, and I am so grateful for the best editor in the world. I love and admire you, Judy! Barbara and Bob are more than mere publishers, they are dear friends. I feel extremely fortunate to work with High Country Publishers!

--Lila Hopkins

For

Jeanne

in gratitude for her faithful and steadfast
care of our precious mother;
and for

Joyce and Leland,

who join me in saying thanks to

Our Incomparable Sister

Strike a Golden Chord

by

Lila Hopkins

The Gilded Teapot
9 a.m. – 5 p.m.
The Gilded Teapot

♫

Chapter One

She was already late, and now the stupid key wouldn't turn. Joanna Jerome – the cool, calm, competent Joanna – was on the verge of losing it. She couldn't think; she couldn't get to work on time; she couldn't even unlock the door. She had kidded about her sanity during the last two years, but maybe it wasn't a joke.

She pursed her lips, jammed the key into the lock again, and shoved. The door slammed back against the wall and she nearly fell into the storeroom. She caught herself on a large box and straightened up, glanced at the wall clock and grimaced. It might be usual for some people to be late by seven minutes, but this twenty-eight-year-old was punctual and dependable always – until today. The rain had slowed her, surely, but she should have allowed more time.

She hung her dripping umbrella by the door. If she wasn't losing her mind, how could she explain this strange craziness that had stalked her all morning – an eerie feeling of tingly expectation? This was wild.

She checked to make sure she hadn't crushed the corner of the box she fell against and stepped gingerly around several large packages, delivered just before closing last night. Ordinarily, she would have ripped the boxes open, eager to check out the beautiful Wedgwood porcelain, but she was too tired last night to linger.

The room was stuffy, so she flipped on the switch of the dehumidifier, producing a familiar reassuring hum, yet she couldn't conquer a strange uneasiness. She took a quick glance around the rest of the storeroom and moved into the salesroom. The showcases of china – rows of pale rounded shapes of teapots and cups touched with bright colors, the faces of the tiny pottery animals peeking from among the porcelain – all seemed as it should be. The three small tables where she served her customers exotic teas and cookies, each with its crystal bud vase of late summer asters. Nothing looked disturbed. The drawers where she stored linens looked disgustingly normal.

Am I expecting mysterious drama on this wet fall morning in my quiet little shop and tea room? An armed robbery, perhaps? A camera-team of reporters from Sixty Minutes? Nonsense! She had one wild imagination. Joanna had left that sort of thing behind when she moved to Galax Falls, North Carolina, high in the Blue Ridge Mountains.

I'm just being theatrical. There's no room in my life for this craziness, and I simply won't allow it. She bit her lip, and calmed herself. In the huge mirror over the counter, her dark brown hair, neatly brushed into a French twist, looked no worse for the wind and rain. She studied herself a minute; she didn't look crazy. In fact, she admitted, she wasn't bad looking. She couldn't be, if she really looked like her handsome brother, as people suggested.

It wasn't a sense of apprehension she was experiencing, but an unfamiliar feeling of anticipation, as though something wonderful was about to happen. That would be interesting, she thought. She could handle a little excitement, for a change.

Sliding her purse under the counter, Joanna hurried to open her little establishment. She noticed a bare place on the wall and felt a little start until she remembered that she had sold one of Lila's paintings yesterday. The memory of the retired teacher's excitement about the sale made her smile.

I act as if I'm expecting a horde of customers. She leaned down to grasp the door shade. It was usually mid-morning before her first patron wandered in. She pulled lightly on the shade and, maintaining just enough pressure, steered it up nearly halfway to find herself staring at a pair of scuffed men's oxfords and jeans. She concentrated on the image outside the glass door.

Just my luck to leave a customer waiting the first time I'm late.

She raised the shade higher.

A man crouched in front of the door, rain streaming down his cheeks. His eyes squinted at her just above the neatly gold-lettered sign:

The masculine face rose as she stretched to her tiptoes above the sign.

Joanna froze, and the man did too. She straightened her shoulders, and he squared his.

She felt disconcerted, uncustomarily nervous. His movements seemed a mirrored counterpart of hers, but nothing in his manner indicated derision as he solemnly concentrated on her activity.

But why was he there? Hers was mostly a woman's establishment, selling fine porcelain and linens – not much to interest a man, except maybe the old books and tapes.

His intense brown eyes were on a level with hers, now.

Her fingers trembled. Nine inches from the top the shade stuck. She pulled gently to nudge it up, but it didn't budge. Frustrated, she jerked it, and the roller and shade crashed to the floor. She sputtered in embarrassment.

The stranger watched intently, but didn't laugh.

She could have released the spring-loaded foot lock with her toe, but she stooped to unlock it manually, to give herself time to regain her composure.

Observing as she pressed the release, the man turned his ear to the click when the lock disengaged. She rose to insert the key into the main lock, and he stood to his full height. She fumbled with her keys, almost dropping them, inserted the wrong one, jerked it out of the lock, and jammed in another. The key would not turn. What was it about her and locks today?

She gave a deep sigh, avoiding the brown eyes that studied her through the glass door. In spite of the steady drizzle that plastered his hair against his forehead and soaked his plaid shirt, he waited patiently. He didn't seem annoyed, nor did he laugh at her.

On the third attempt she finally inserted the right key. The lock turned, and with deep relief she opened the door.

He stepped quickly across the threshold and stood before her, dripping rainwater on her new floor mat.

Joanna caught her breath.

Together they said, "I'm sorry . . ."

" . . . about the floor," he added.

" . . . about being late," she murmured.

They both laughed.

"Would you like some tea?" she asked. She hadn't had time to prepare it yet, but he looked cold.

"No, thanks. I'll tell you why I'm here."

He shook his arms, and rainwater pelted her. "I'm sorry. I didn't mean to drown you. My old dog Charlie used to do that – when I took him for walks in the rain. I thought he did it just to aggravate me."

She felt uneasy under his scrutiny as she brushed some of the rainwater from her hair, reminding him that she was already wet.

He said, almost as to himself, "I'll bet you like to take long walks in the rain."

She smiled. He was, after all, a customer – a potential customer, anyway. *What makes some men so arrogant? I've had my fill of that type.* Actually taking long walks in the rain sounded like a glorious, romantic thing to do on a nice warm day, but she wouldn't admit it to this man whose name she didn't know.

She had been fooled by his athletic build, judging him to be of college age. Up close he looked older than the rain-blurred face that had lurked outside the door. His large nose and square jaw rescued his face from being classically handsome. He had a friendly mouth, poised for a smile, it seemed. That put her more at ease, but she was wary of that flirtatious velvet voice.

"The movers lost a box of my favorite cassettes," he said, "and my landlady said you'd be the only one in town who might have the ones I'm looking for."

He glanced at her wet hair, a sympathetic smile hovering around his lips. He was saturated by the storm, his shirt clinging to broad shoulders.

I'll remain impervious to his charm, she determined, feeling as self-conscious as a convent schoolgirl in her first encounter with the opposite sex.

"I hate to disappoint you, but I have only a few old tapes. The owner of the building left them, along with some boxes of old books. You're welcome to go through them. I'll show you." She led him to the far side of a counter. "I haven't the space to display them and haven't had time to sort through the books."

She pointed toward a small stool, and he pulled it toward the tapes, settling down with an expectant sigh, then focused on the tapes. She watched him a moment and when he didn't look up again, she felt that he had dismissed her.

Reluctantly, she returned to the front counter, brushed water from her raincoat, and was unbuttoning it when the front door slammed back against the wall.

"Edward!"

Edward Westmoreland maneuvered an oversized blue-and-orange golf umbrella into the shop, cradling a huge bouquet of peach-colored roses wrapped in green tissue paper. He sported a classic trench coat and rain hat. His plastic-framed glasses had slipped down on his nose, giving him the appearance of an overdressed owl.

Joanna reached for the umbrella, but he yanked it back and thrust the flowers toward her.

"I was rude and domineering last night." He used his middle finger to push his glasses back up on his nose. "I deserve another chance. It took me some time to locate the Virginia Roses that have the fragrance you like."

"Ed," she said, and took a deep breath, "I don't like to be rude either, but my answer holds. I'm sorry."

He stared at her. A scowl crossed his broad forehead.

"Give me time," he insisted. "I came on too strong. I'm aggressive and often too forceful. Joanna, I want you to be my wife. Please."

She studied the floor and saw the muddy puddle spreading, soaking the welcome mat and sloshing against his polished black shoes. The overpowering fragrance of the roses dominated the small space. She felt like tossing them back, but he leaned the umbrella against the door facing and folded his arms across his chest.

Romance was not his forte.

Pompous ass.

"We'll discuss it later." With the tip of his umbrella he nudged the roller and shade on the floor. "Better fix that. A customer could trip over it, and you'd have a lawsuit on your hands."

A rebuttal stuck in her throat as he frowned, checked his watch, and said tersely, "I'm late for court. I'll come take you to lunch."

"No, Ed."

He adjusted his glasses, pulled his hat low over his eyes, and stepped outside to ease open the umbrella, totally disregarding her refusal.

What am I to do with dozens of roses in this cramped space? "Men!" she spat out in disgust. *I'll take the roses to my dad at lunchtime.* She would close the shop and wouldn't be here when Ed returned.

Hunting a container for water, she was startled by a diplomatic cough. *Good heavens!* She had forgotten her customer.

He heard it all! She knew her face must be turning crimson.

"Er . . . ah, I found some cassettes that I want," he said, "but I'm far more interested in the books. Did you know that you have some valuable volumes here?"

He was gracious enough to not mention her visitor.

"I know there are some first editions."

"You don't have them priced."

"I have no idea what they're worth."

"Old books are a hobby of mine," he said. "Let me do a little research."

As she fumbled with the tissue paper around the unwieldy bouquet, she wondered if she was still blushing. She hated being embarrassed.

"Don't you like roses?" he asked, his voice steady but his eyes dancing with merriment, his lips twitching with repressed laughter.

"Are you making fun of me?"

"No. Just thinking of the consternation in your boyfriend's voice. Perhaps he should have chosen violets." He placed several cassettes on the counter, including *My Fair Lady*.

"I am not Eliza Doolittle," Joanna informed him, "and he isn't my boyfriend."

"Well, he either has been, or badly wants to be. You don't seem to think much of men."

His voice carried an irritating tone of indifference that belied the teasing mischief in his eyes. "Can I help you with your raincoat?" he asked as he stepped uninvited behind the counter.

She had chosen the yellow coat to complement her dark eyes and hair, but as she turned her back to him, she felt garish, self-conscious. He slid the raincoat off her shoulders and hung it on a hook behind the door, then slid his wallet from the back pocket of his jeans.

"How much do I owe you?" He brushed the hair back from his forehead, and she noticed that it dried to the color of sand.

Joanna's hand was unsteady as she added the tab. "I'm glad you found something you like. What kind of tapes did you lose?"

He tapped the cassettes rhythmically against the edge of the counter.

"Oh, Vivaldi . . . Tchaikovsky." Raising his eyes to the ceiling, he seemed to be listening to the music. "My favorites were Bach and Handel's organ concertos."

A tickling of pleasure rippled through her. She smiled. "I like those also."

His boyish grin made him look years younger.

"Really? Great." He pulled a small notebook from his shirt pocket and tore a page from it. "I'm Russell Benenson, the new English teacher at the high school. Here's my phone number." He leaned over the counter to scrawl a number on the sheet.

So why did she need his phone number? She shared his taste in music, but . . .

"Hope you won't sell those books until you hear from me. If you get a buyer, would you please call me before you let them go?"

She nodded. He seemed relieved. She certainly was. "Mr. Ben . . ." She paused to look at his handwriting. "Mr. Benenson – "

"Ben. Call me Ben. Everyone does."

"I'm – Joanna Jerome." Her face felt hot.

"Joanna Jerome," he repeated, pronouncing it in a deep, resonant bass. "Musical."

"Would you like a cup of tea now?"

"I'm not much of a tea drinker, but it smells wonderful in here. Almost enticing enough to get me to try some tea."

"Coffee?"

His eyes brightened with interest, and he nodded. She felt weak behind her knees and knew she was clinging to an excuse to keep him in the shop for a while.

"I'm afraid it will have to be . . . instant," she said. "The coffee pot is broken. Is that okay?"

"Blah!" He shuddered, headed for the door, and turned around grinning. "Anyway, I mustn't be around when Romeo comes to take you to lunch."

She made a face at his retreating back, feeling so frustrated that she would have liked to throw something at him. At the moment though, the only thing available was the dumb bouquet of roses and lots of very expensive porcelain.

"Ben," she called behind him, "don't you have an umbrella?"

"Umbrella? Not my style. I love walking in the rain. My mother told me a long time ago that my skin is waterproof. You need a gentle summer rain to produce rain dust."

"Rain dust? What's that?"

"You don't know about rain dust? I'll tell you about it some time."

He paused at the door, shoved his cassette tapes into his pocket, picked up the shade and roller, adjusted the brackets, and deftly rehung it, then raised the shade.

"We don't want a lawsuit on our hands," he said and turned to salute her. "See you later, Joanna Jerome."

♫

♫

Chapter Two

"Jo?" Her father had fallen asleep in his reading chair and woke with a start. "I didn't know you were coming home for lunch, honey."

"I wanted to bring you these," she said.

He sat up and rubbed his eyes, looking at the roses. "You didn't go and buy – ?"

"No. They're from Ed."

"Oh." There had always been a special communication between them, and she didn't need to explain.

"Has Mrs. Campbell been here?" she asked.

"Yes. She fixed me a sandwich. We'll eat together." He pulled back the afghan that covered his legs and reached for his walker. Knowing not to assist him unless he asked, she went to the kitchen to find a vase.

"Dad," she called to him, "I had a customer waiting when I arrived at the shop this morning."

"Did she buy a lot?"

He pulled out a chair and sat down awkwardly at the table.

"It was a man who was interested in the old

books Mr. Henry left, but I don't know how to price them." She hoped he would ask questions. She wanted to tell him about Ben, wanted to describe his rugged good looks and his patience about standing in the rain until she could unlock the shop. Her dad would laugh if she told about the door shade falling and causing such a ruckus.

When he showed no interest, she said, "I'll stop by the church after work to practice, but I'll come home before choir rehearsal."

"Fine. That's hardly the quality of the organ you played in Raleigh, but . . ." He had developed the habit of starting a sentence and not finishing it.

"I love the organ here, Dad. Mom taught me to play it, and I feel close to her there."

He patted her hand, and his felt cold. When he finished his sandwich, he said, "I'd like to lie down. I'll watch Court TV in the den, and it'll put me to sleep." He smiled wanly, and she stood to help him. "No, no! Eat your lunch, Jo. Don't feel you must always check on me." He hesitated in the doorway. "Ed is coming over this evening to go over some briefs. I'll have him stop by the drive-in and bring some barbecue for the two of us. You can just eat downtown and save yourself a trip."

"Okay." She tried to mask her pain in witnessing his shuffling pace.

"Ed might not be husband material," he said, "but he is an excellent lawyer. Remember that if you ever need an attorney. He attends to details, and . . ." His voice trailed off again.

"Thanks, Dad. I'll remember." She was genuinely glad he was pleased with Ed's work.Her dad deserved a competent partner.

♫ ♫ ♫

Life had taken an unexpected twist when it transported Joanna back to Galax Falls. As much as she loved the Blue Ridge Mountains and Avery County, she had thought her lifetime niche was in Raleigh. She never dreamed that she would come back – and open a gift shop at that!

When she first talked about opening the shop, her mother's closest friend and still a valued confidant, Patsy Adams, offered to make tablecloths and napkins. The cloths were checkered drip-dry synthetics, with solid napkins to match. Patsy made several sets in different colors: blue, green, pink and yellow, so Joanna could change them for different seasons. Patsy taught her to fold the napkins in the rosebud pattern, a favorite style her mother loved to use at dinner parties.

But she missed the activities of the city. She had delighted in her work at the university, and being organist at the Dovewing Community Church was something to which she had aspired most of her adulthood. She presented concerts for several years that were the highlights of her life. Still, she had no choice. Her dad needed her.

The Raleigh church found a replacement quickly, and within a week Ken Hoffman, the choral director, was escorting another fair lady around the city. It occurred to her that perhaps she had not belonged there after all.

Still the adjustment to coming home was traumatic. The pain of watching her father's body being wrecked by ALS, Lou Gehrig's Disease, was almost more than she could stand. So many times she woke, weeping, from dreams of her mother – wishing she were there to comfort both of them. If her mother were still alive, Joanna wouldn't have had to abandon her dreams . . . *No! I simply will not let myself think like that!* she vowed.

That she enjoyed Ben's visit so much underlined the dearth of her current social life. Many of her high school friends had moved away and others were busy with family. Her own life revolved around caring for her father and keeping the little shop running smoothly.

She thought about Ben's pleasing laugh, remembered his gorgeous brown eyes and wavy hair – but he had overheard Ed and clearly enjoyed the little drama. Her stomach churned with embarrassment. This man created conflicting responses in her, certainly.

♬ ♬ ♬

The church was beautiful in the late afternoon. She loved being there. The weathered rock structure provided a safe haven, insulating her from life's disappointments as surely as it shut out traffic noise. The light through the stained glass windows, brilliant on sunny Sunday mornings, was muted, softened by the late afternoon, and the building seemed dark. For Joanna, the sanctuary was filled with ethereal peace.

The scent of candles helped to dispel the musty odor of the antique fabrics, and containers of greenery provided a fresh fragrance. It was an old church, perhaps only one-fifth as large as the one in Raleigh. The pews, over a hundred years old, were crafted from wormy chestnut and had a rich, reddish glow. The vaulted ceiling drew her eyes upward, deep into the shadows that she knew were only an illusion of a barrier between herself and the eternal.

Taking a deep breath, she imagined her

mother at the organ. She had been Joanna's first music teacher. At least her death was quick, unlike her father's lingering muscle degeneration disease.

"I miss you, Mother."

Joanna moved down the aisle in the darkened church, reaching down to brush the pew backs, her footsteps echoing on the slate floor. For a moment, the echoes brought back memories of high school, of basketball games where she led the freshman team as forward. They all said she could have been an athlete. But Mother refused to allow her to compromise on dual allegiances, and Joanna made her choice. All her vitality stayed focused on music.

Though her mother never tolerated arrogance, she helped Joanna develop pride in her mastery of technique. Wonder grabbed her each time she approached the organ. Her spine straightened as confidence flowed into her, and she strode with dignity to the instrument. She stepped up to the console and caressed the polished dark wood.

"You have been blessed with a gift," her father often reminded her. "Use it for your Maker's glory."

In the semidarkness she bent over to remove her street shoes and to step into the black organ ones. As she adjusted the straps, she recalled Saturday-morning shopping trips with her mother as a young student. Now she ordered her shoes from a music supply house, but not twenty years ago. "Mary Jane shoes," her mother told the clerk. "Inch-and-a-half heels – and leather soles, very thin."

She explained to her daughter, "Patent leather sticks together."

Joanna knew from experience that she would find strength in routine tasks, so she went to work, unlocking the organ, activating the power switch, and sliding onto the bench before snapping on the light. She found herself trembling as she reached for her music.

Then she flashed on an unexpected memory.

She saw herself in a white evening pantsuit. Spotlights caught her in the wings and followed as she walked across a concert stage.

Thunderous applause heralded her entry, then abated politely, and the auditorium became hushed as she seated herself at the console of a grand pipe organ.

The house lights slowly dimmed.

Joanna felt, again, the expectation of the audience, her own excitement . . .

♫ ♫ ♫

Now her shoulders sagged, and for a fleeting moment she grieved for the career that had crash-landed. Her concert days were probably over, she reminded herself as she fingered the gold medallion that hung from the chain around her neck. Still, that life must be balanced against the opportunity to care for her father.

Usually she began her practice with warm-up procedures, and something calming, like Brahms, but tonight she started by sorting through her music with an unaccustomed frenzy. Ben had said his favorites were Bach and Handel's organ concertos.

She changed the registration, opting for an abrupt shift in plans.

Bach's *G Minor Fantasy* – the fiery notes swelled to envelop her. Energy surged through her – as though the electricity that enlivened the organ somehow flowed to her fingertips. The impetuous, triumphant composition of the master filled the small chapel, its deep rich tones transforming it into a magnificent cathedral. The passion of the music lifted her, inspired her, and obliterated her loneliness. She worked on several parts, repeating, perfecting her technique, and then she played it through again. The music swelled in a riveting crescendo to its climactic resolution.

Emotionally drained, she dropped her hands to her lap. Not even aware of her actions, she reached up and released the French twist in her hair, letting it fall to her shoulders. Relaxed, she rested momentarily and worked briefly with the stops again before turning to the soothing works of Brahms and Mendelssohn. Finally she practiced Maurice Durufle's *Veni Creator*.

She didn't know how long she played. She forgot everything that threatened her happiness . . . her father's health . . . the shop . . . Ed . . . the stranger who had thrown her emotions into a turmoil . . .

Suddenly the overhead lights switched on, and like a blare of a raucous horn, boisterous laughter and conversation shattered the tranquility. Joanna gasped. She hadn't realized how dark the sanctuary had become, how late the hour, or that others had arrived.

The choir director, Mr. Hughes, greeted her. "Sounds terrific. I haven't heard the organ sing like that in years. Been here long?"

He opened his briefcase and began to arrange his music. Several choir members spoke to her as they moved to their assigned seats . . . and then she saw Ben.

Her heart lurched.

"A new member for the choir," Mr. Hughes said. "Marvelous baritone. I knew him in Winston-Salem and lost no time contacting him when I heard he was moving here. Ben, come meet our organist, Joanna Jerome."

Ben bowed slightly and shook her hand. "Joanna Jerome. Joanna of The Gilded Teapot that doesn't serve coffee."

She laughed, and her cheeks burned. *Tomorrow I'm buying a new coffee pot.*

Mr. Hughes chuckled then turned back to his music.

Ben said, "I've been huddled back there in the dark, listening. I heard only the last of the *Fantasy.* When you played Mendelssohn, I almost applauded, but I was afraid I'd blow my cover and you might stop playing. I waited, and you rewarded me with . . . what was it? Oh, I don't know the name of the composer, but you surely got a workout on the pedal work. Wow!"

He left her speechless as he turned and followed Mr. Hughes to the choir loft.

Will I be able to play? Her hands trembled, and her knees shook. She couldn't keep her feet steady on the pedals. *I'm a professional. I won't allow myself to be affected by flattery.*

She put her trust in her skills, and prayed for strength. Years of diligent training kicked in, and no one would have guessed the pandemonium that raged within her.

Concentrate on the director and the music.

She had been with far better choirs and worked under master directors, but tonight the music sprouted wings, and the rehearsal had majesty and magic.

Joanna was exhausted, and the choir was breathless when Mr. Hughes finally dismissed the choir. The celestial echo of the music still lingered when the squeal of a toddler sounded as the fair-haired cherub tottered down the aisle toward the choir loft. Ben, interrupted en route to Joanna, turned to greet the child.

"Hey, Benjie! Come on down, boy. I want you to meet a friend."

He scooped the boy into his arms and waved at someone just beyond Joanna's line of vision. Following the direction of his glance, she saw that several people had filtered into the building, waiting for choir members. She watched as Ben hurried to an attractive blonde, and all the energy drained from her.

The child put his arms around Ben's neck. "Mr. Hughes, you remember Beth. And this is our Benjie."

Joanna could not remember locking the organ. She assumed she had secured her music and turned off the light. Slipping quickly out the side door and across the wet pavement to her car, she realized she had forgotten to change her shoes. The organ shoes were soggy and likely ruined.

How could I have been so stupid? She wanted to scream at herself. *Of course he'd have a wife! What a fool I made of myself!* Her only consolation was that she had not shared the information of her attraction to Ben. No one else need ever know about the pain she felt tonight. She would put this day – this day she had expected something wonderful to happen – behind her, and never think of it again.

She would be strong. She would be the dependable, unruffled Joanna Jerome that Nicholas often called her.

♫

Chapter Three

Dazzling morning sunshine sharply contrasted Joanna's dark mood, but she would simply refuse to think about Ben and her ridiculous infatuation. She drove another block.

"I'll bet you like to take long walks in the rain." His voice had *seemed* friendly. *"You don't seem to think much of men."*

She chewed on her lip, trying to push away the memories. It wasn't fair. He walked into her shop, spent no more than twenty minutes, and unleashed havoc with her emotions.

I'm becoming paranoid. She struggled with the void in her life. *Will I be stranded in this little mountain town with no opportunity to meet a man I could really share my life with? Could I end up marrying Ed?* She shuddered. *No!*

She remembered Ben's sputtered, *"Blah!"* at the suggestion of instant coffee. Finally she just gave in and reviewed everything he said to her; every nuance in his demeanor; the way he smiled, pronounced her name, loved her kind of music. He didn't actually touch her when he helped with her coat, but she was acutely aware of his presence behind her.

"See you later, Joanna Jerome."

The memories played across her consciousness like a favorite song, repeating itself over and over as she entered the empty shop. She usually enjoyed the early hours before customers came in – several regulars who stopped for coffee, especially when her dad was there. Today, she was restless and didn't want to work on the new display she was planning.

She glanced at her reflection. She had not taken time to brush her hair into the French twist this morning, but it felt heavy on her neck. After scavenging around under the counter for a rubber band and stretching it around her wrist, she gathered her hair as though making a ponytail. Then she deftly pulled the hair through the rubber band, stopping just before forming a ponytail. It wasn't elegant but kept her hair in a neat bun.

I'm acting like a moonstruck adolescent. Why didn't I notice a wedding ring when he took money out of his wallet, or when he wrote down his phone number? Surely I would have seen a slender gold band . . .

Yesterday, before leaving the shop for organ practice, she had planned to remove the books Ben admired. She placed sturdy boxes on the floor next to them. *Tomorrow,* she had promised herself, *I'll store them away and keep them safe for him.*

This morning, however, she pushed the boxes out of the way and brushed past the books without a glance in their direction. She marched to the front door and raised the blind, noting dispassionately that no roguish interloper lay in wait outside the door. She walked away, then stopped, grabbed a small bell out of a display case, and retraced her steps to the door.

Nobody intrudes on me today without warning.

♫ ♫ ♫

Joanna was not a typical entrepreneur. Because she needed a low-pressure diversion from the care of her father, she opened her tea and gift shop on an impulse after she visited one in Santa Barbara, California, that featured live music.

She chose a place near her father's law offices and arranged a comfortable reading space for him, hoping that he would slip away from work occasionally to visit and rest. She found a storefront that had originally been a drug store, but most recently Mr. Henry's antique shop. A high counter hid a sink, small refrigerator and hotplate, perfect for her tea preparation. In addition to the attractive salesroom, there was one nice storeroom in the back, plus a smaller room with a closet, a restroom and place for her office.

Nicholas seemed delighted to have her home and expressed considerable pride in her shop, and until recently, spent an hour or two there most afternoons. She provided him with a leather recliner, a reading light and a table for his books. He, in return, kept a standing weekly order of fresh flowers, which she arranged for each of the serving tables. It had torn her heart out when he sent someone by to pick up the chair after he stopped practicing law.

She had no room for a concert organ, and no time to play it, so she installed a stereo system to play her favorite classical music. Her inventory featured ceramics, an interest developed by her mother, an excellent potter herself, who had taught her to appreciate glaze and form. Joanna and her father still owned many lovely pieces made by her mother.

Mother and daughter shared a passion for fine china and were delighted by the translucency of a Lenox cup or a Mikasa saucer. They were fascinated by the use of ultraviolet light for detecting repairs, restoration and fakes. It was easy for her to choose what she wanted to sell: fine china, a few antiques and some crafts. She found an excellent supplier of china in Greensboro, and she bought from the former owner the entire inventory of the antique merchandise, the last remnants of stock, including a variety of glassware, linens, books, and a few toys. To these she added the whimsical animals and exquisite table fountains handcrafted by Cindy Pacileo–much to the delight of Nicholas.

She served tea and cookies at three small tables near the windows, and the place was especially popular with retired ladies in the community. Everything about the shop reminded her of her mother – from the cut glass vases that matched crystal sets for sugar and cream to the little silver dish she used for packets of sugar substitutes.

She had always enjoyed Galax Falls' small business district, gift and craft shops, and a few small cafes that profited from a brisk summer business when tourists crowded into the mountains. Her shop gave local artists a chance to display their work.

By three o'clock that day she was fighting a fatigue that could give way to depression if she let it. She could not remember a single thing she did all day or recall the face of one customer. She had worked mechanically, almost as if being operated by remote control.

She brewed a fresh pot of tea, reloaded the compact-disk player, and had just begun to nibble on a confection from her supply of cookie tins when she heard the little bell jingle. A young woman shoved the door open and pushed a heavy stroller into the shop.

Joanna froze momentarily, unable to react. Any other time she would have helped maneuver the cumbersome stroller into the shop. *It was her – Ben's wife – it had to be.*

She caught her breath as she looked down at the small boy being lifted from the stroller, and she was startled by his mother's pixie-like youthfulness. She wore form-fitting bleached blue jeans, a striped cotton shirt, and sandals. Something about her was familiar. *Ben never introduced us last night; when could we have met?*

The newcomer paused to brush a strand of short blonde hair back over her right ear, glanced inquisitively around the shop, then said with an impish grin, "Isn't Barnes and Noble, that's for sure."

The child swayed slightly, steadied himself, and headed toward the counter to stare up at Joanna. She looked into huge brown eyes. "You must be Benjie," she said in a faltering voice, staring at his curly blond hair.

He was about two years old. He gave her an engaging smile, his gaze lingered on her cookie, and he pointed to it with a stubby finger.

"Would you like a cookie?" Joanna asked.

"Benjie!" his mother exclaimed.

The child had already raised his hands toward the tray that Joanna lowered to him. He grabbed a fistful of cookies in each hand.

"One cookie, Benjamin. Take one cookie," he was instructed again by his mother.

Obediently he dropped several, but he looked

at Joanna with such a wistful expression that she laughed in spite of the confusing emotions that swirled through her. Still he clutched one cookie in each fist. "Have two cookies, Benjie."

"Oh, I'm so sorry. I'll pay for them."

"No problem. Only a few left in this tin. You have one too." Joanna realized why the young woman looked so familiar. Her smile was a duplicate of Ben's.

"I'm Beth Morgan. My brother started classes today, and he wanted me to get an inventory of your books."

"Your . . . your brother?"

"I think he came in here yesterday. Russell Benenson. Ben. Isn't this where he found some old books?" She turned quickly to check the name on the glass door. "He said they were at a nice little tea shop downtown."

"Yes. He, ah . . . he did. Ben . . . your brother came here." Joanna hoped the remarkable new timbre in her voice would not give her away.

"Of course this is the shop," Beth said, "'cause he said you were one elegant lady. I saw you at choir practice last night! He bragged about your playing all through breakfast!"

It started then, the song in Joanna's heart, as a quiet chord, *pianissimo*, then shifted into flowing trills that grew into a lilting anthem, *fortissimo*. Until this moment she had not noticed that the afternoon sunlight was dancing through the windows. She leaned toward Beth and whispered as though they were in a delightful conspiracy, "Even if I didn't serve coffee?"

A giggle rippled from Beth.

"He's kinda nuts about his coffee, among

other things," she said, and grew serious suddenly. "Can I ask you a personal question?"

Joanna squirmed. "Could I stop you?" Her cheeks were growing warm.

Beth studied Joanna's face, and her gaze lingered on Joanna's brown hair.

Joanna immediately regretted her earlier haste in not brushing it into a French twist. She felt sloppy and was tempted to reach up and yank the rubber band out.

"I have read – not that I spend much time with beauty magazines or care what they say – but I read that only the truly beautiful can wear their hair pulled back in a severe bun like that."

Joanna touched her face at the hair line. Was she going to tell her she was an impostor, wearing a "for beautiful only" hair style?

Beth continued. "I guess that is why it looks so great on you. What I wonder is . . . how do you do it and is my hair long enough to try it? It looks *so* cool."

Joanna blushed. *What a charming little creature you are, Beth.* "Your hair is probably not long enough, but when I am not at work, expecting customers, I'll gladly show you!"

"Good, then I have another question." Joanna braced herself but Beth brought her back down to earth. "D'you have any herbal tea? These cookies are sorta dry."

♫

♫

Chapter Four

"So," Beth rattled on as Joanna brought two cups of herbal tea to the table: "Why is someone with your talent holing up in this hick town?"

Joanna gulped as the banter continued. The recordings of Tchaikovsky's piano overtures seemed out of place. Benjie had climbed down from his mother and hurried to Joanna's opened arms. She lifted him onto her lap.

"I told my brother that you left Raleigh because of some love scandal, 'cause you are too pretty." Beth paused to smooth a strand of hair behind her ear. "But Ben didn't think so. Oh, not that you aren't pretty," she squealed, "but that you were involved in a scandal!"

Joanna felt her face burning. The suggestion about a scandal made her angry for some ridiculous reason. "And you, Beth. You are in this quaint little village because of a scandal?"

"Yes."

That was not what Joanna expected. She didn't know what to say.

Abruptly changing the subject, Beth said, "I

ran a small catering business in Winston-Salem. If I stay up here with Ben, I'll bake you some pastries that will put your business on the map." She leaned across the table to wipe cookie crumbs from her son's chin.

Joanna's anger dissipated. Suddenly the girl's audacity was refreshing and amusing. She burst out laughing and had to put down her cup to keep from spilling her tea.

Benjie pulled his head back from her and stared, perplexed. He grinned, then mimicked her by laughing too.

Beth looked at her in bewilderment.

"You're right," Joanna said, pausing to brush tears from her cheeks, unable to remember when she had laughed so hard. "These cookies *are* horrible."

"Wrong baking powder."

"I guess so. I didn't bake them."

Suddenly serious, Beth said, "Please don't tell Ben what I said. He thinks I'm rude."

"Where does he get that idea?" Joanna asked, struggling to maintain a deadpan expression.

"See that man?" Beth pointed outside. "Who is he? He's so incredibly handsome."

Ed was striding across the street, briefcase in hand. At least he was not carrying flowers.

"The one in the dark gray suit? That's Ed Westmoreland, my dad's law partner."

"He's headed here! He looks like a young Jimmy Stewart – didn't you just love Jimmy Stewart in *The Philadelphia Story*? With Katherine Hepburn and Cary Grant? I have a copy of that film! Ben gave it to me for Christmas." Beth rattled on. "I saw that guy at the drugstore, and everybody was treating him like he's some kind of nobleman. That's some snappy fedora. Great target for a snowball."

Joanna eased Benjie out of her lap and lowered the volume on the stereo before she turned to greet Ed, who glanced at the lone customer, acknowledged her presence with a nod, and solemnly removed his "snappy" hat.

He said to Joanna, "I brought some papers for you to take to your father."

He walked to the counter and laid his briefcase on it, then pushed his glasses into a better position on his nose. Beth stared at him, speechless, her eyes large circles of incredulity.

Joanna cleared a space for the papers. She was not in the habit of introducing her customers and was undecided about doing it now. Her gaze fell on Benjie as he tottered toward the counter.

Ed was watching the child nervously, as though he was being cornered by a bulldog. His awkward attempt to smile was pathetic.

Benjie stared at him quizzically, then wrapped his arms around one leg.

Ed stiffened. He turned pale when Beth admonished her son, "Benjamin, don't slobber all over the man's trousers." Ed gave Joanna a wide-eyed plea for help, and his right leg began shaking. A cobra wrapped around his leg would not have caused more consternation.

In her hurry to scramble from the table, Beth knocked over her cup of tea. She picked up her napkin, looked at it and dropped it on the table. "Don't you have any paper napkins?" she asked as she scurried to Benjie. She had to pry his arms from Ed's leg. "He's too dad-blamed friendly. Looking for a daddy, I guess." She picked up her son, and her voice trembled as she added, "I think lawyers are absolutely awesome."

She stood slightly behind him, and Ed turned to stare down at her, his eyebrows raised in astonishment, his face pink with discomfort. She said, "Maybe that's just because a smart lawyer sent my ex to jail for spousal abuse."

Benjie reached toward him, his hands dusted with cookie crumbs. Ed drew back. His glasses slid down his nose a quarter of an inch.

"Benjie, darling," Beth said, "he's not your daddy. I'm sorry, but he isn't. He looks like a very nice man, and I'll bet he never hit a woman in his life."

Without a word Ed hastened toward the door. He hesitated and shot a worried glance at Benjie and Beth.

"Ed!" Joanna called. "You forgot your hat."

He avoided eye contact with her and shoved the hat down low over his eyes.

Joanna saw that Ben's sister had pegged Ed's personality and was enjoying his embarrassment.

"Benjie," Beth said in a stage whisper, "maybe you'll become a *gen-tal-man* like that. He's plumb aristocratic." She reached around the counter, grabbed a roll of paper towels and returned to the table to mop up the spilled tea, her back to the departing Ed. "Wow!" she exclaimed. "He's one handsome devil."

Ed froze for a split second with his hand on the doorknob. His ears turned scarlet before he nearly knocked down the door in his escape.

Joanna remained rooted at the counter, mouth gaping open. "You did that on purpose!"

"Sure." She was a mischievous sprite, thoroughly enjoying herself.

"He was terribly embarrassed," Joanna said.

"The man's too uptight. I'll bet that deep inside he kinda liked being called handsome."

Joanna shook her head. Ed Westmoreland did *not* enjoy the teasing – Joanna was sure of it.

In spite of the way Beth harassed Ed, Joanna was captivated by the young creature who walked into her shop and snatched control of her most private emotions. "Beth, some time you must tell me all about your interesting life."

♬ ♬ ♬

When Joanna related the incident to her father, he laughed so hard that he had to brush tears from his cheeks.

"Jo, I'd give a month's income to have been there."

"Oh, Dad, I wanted to scream with laughter. Ed was an absolute basket case. Acted scared to death of a little kid."

"Probably never been that close to one before!" Then he surprised her. "Beth might be just what Ed needs." He raised his hand to silence her protest. "No, I mean it. I know him better than you do. I've worked with the man for four years, and I've met his parents. They're so uptight and prudish, they act like having a good time of any kind is sinful. He's a good man, but he needs someone to help him break out of that stuffy mold. Perhaps she can loosen him up a little. I've got to meet this young lady!"

"I hope you'll meet her brother."

"I may have already. One day this summer a teacher came into the office and had us write up a restraining order to protect his sister. I was impressed. A nice-looking young man, about six feet tall with broad shoulders?"

"And laughing brown eyes." Joanna was thinking about his reference to Ed as 'Romeo.' "He joined the choir," she said.

"Did he? Terrific. That should make your life more interesting."

He studied her, and she felt her cheeks burning. "I thought Beth was his wife when she first came into the shop," she said, and twisted her hands.

"That must have been disappointing. You don't plan to elope this week, do you, honey?"

"Dad!" She crossed the room to put her arm around him and lean her face against his. "He may not be interested in me at all."

"Well, he would be mighty stupid if he isn't. I'm only teasing – but I'm praying that you'll meet someone really fine while I'm still . . . able to attend the wedding." He kissed her cheek.

Her heart was breaking. "Dad . . ."

♫

Chapter Five

Beth Morgan hadn't intended to share the miserable secrets of her life with anyone, especially a beautiful woman who was as successful and self-confident as Joanna Jerome.

She was intrigued by Ben's sudden interest in The Gilded Teapot, but she had a prickling uncertainty when he described Joanna. A lump formed in her throat. She didn't want to pout – Ben hated it when she pouted – but she fought a wave of jealousy. She had always adored her brother and hoped he would fall in love, but not just yet! He had been enthusiastic about her moving to the mountains with him, but so far she had not agreed to stay in Galax Falls.

It had never occurred to her that, for her sake, Ben would give up his scholarship for doctoral studies in England. Still, when she began receiving anonymous letters threatening her and Benjie, he took them far more seriously than Beth did.

"You're in danger," he said. "I can't leave you."

She begged him to go on to Europe, but he withdrew from the program and applied for work teaching in North Carolina.

"I want you and Benjie out of the city," he said. "We'll go to the mountains."

"I've never been to the mountains, Ben."

He grinned. "Then it's time you went."

She quit arguing with him, though she didn't want him to forsake his studies. She didn't want to move to the mountains, and today she didn't want to run his errand to The Gilded Teapot.

"That's no place for Benjie!" she said. "Not an antique shop."

"It's not really an antique shop," Ben insisted. "Have a cup of tea with Joanna. You can put Benjie in his stroller while you make a list of the books and their publication dates. It'll be days before I can go back there, maybe even weeks."

She put it off until after Benjie's nap. She wished she had one of those new lightweight strollers, but she couldn't complain about the one Ben found in a thrift store. She pushed it toward town, feeling timid and self-conscious. Galax Falls was a high class resort; she was about as out of place as a cat at a wedding reception.

She paused outside the shop and peered nervously through the window, noticing the crisp white curtains appliquéd with gold and blue teapots. *This must be the place . . .*

The young woman behind the counter bore little resemblance to the vivacious woman Beth watched at the organ last night. That woman was full of life, laughing and smiling at the director. Someone who looked as weary as the woman in the shop might resent her dragging in an oversized stroller. She thought about walking on down the street.

The sadness in Joanna's face spoke to her. She knew about sadness.

Come to think of it, several times lately she had caught Ben in an unguarded moment, and his body had showed the same sadness – sagging shoulders, grim lines around the mouth. Beth took a deep breath and pushed the door open, enjoying Benjie's delight in the tinkling silver bell tied to the handle.

Joanna gave her a startled appraisal.

Beth didn't understand what happened, but almost as soon as they entered the shop, the woman's dejection disappeared as surely as a cicada drops its outgrown skin. She supposed it was because of Benjie. Her son had that uplifting effect on people.

Joanna was taller than she expected. Her dark hair had hung loose on her shoulders last night – but today it was tucked into a bun, or a twist or something. Beth liked it better the way it looked last night. Her eyes were the color of brown sugar.

"Come sit down and have a cup of tea," Joanna said, then sat down at the table with them, pulled Benjie onto her lap, and talked with Beth as if they were longtime friends.

It was that moment, when Joanna served her tea, when she knew she wouldn't be returning to the city. Close friendships had been scarce in Beth's life, apart from her relationship with her brother.

♬ ♬ ♬

Ben was the only safe haven Beth Morgan had ever known. Her appearance had been an unwelcome surprise to her mother, who at forty-two thought her childbearing days were over. Beth was an embarrassment to her father, who regarded her with a mixture of bewilderment and a complete lack of interest.

More than ten years older, Ben was the only sibling who even pretended to tolerate her. He was the one who showed her how to dress her dolls, taught her to tie her shoes, and walked her to school on the first day.

She was in the fourth grade, and he was away at college, when her appendix ruptured at school. She begged the school nurse to call her brother instead of her mother, but the law prevailed. Their mother did place a call to Ben's dorm, and he hitchhiked home to spend two nights at the hospital with her while her mother returned to her work as housekeeping supervisor at the Hilton.

By the time she started high school, her other brother and two sisters had long since fled. Beth got into trouble during her first year, arrested with a group of girls in a shoplifting gang. The family practically disowned her – except for Ben, who accompanied her to court and pled for leniency.

He was away at graduate school when she slipped out one night to get married, just to get away from home.

Well, she would tell Ben all about visiting the shop and meeting Joanna, but she wouldn't fill him in about how she mortified that poor young lawyer. One thing was for sure; Mr. Westmoreland would remember her when he saw her again.

You never know, she reminded herself, *when a woman might need a good lawyer.*

♫

Chapter Six

"*Hello!*" His voice was as deep and melodic as she remembered. "Joanna Jerome?"

Why did I remove the warning bell from the door?

She nearly dropped the new coffee pot she was washing and didn't turn to face him, because she couldn't trust her reactions. She had been terribly disappointed when he didn't show up to sing in the choir on Sunday, and the whole episode with him and Beth now seemed like a dream.

"Sorry I missed the music yesterday," he said.

She turned, slowly, and held up the coffee pot. *What would his reaction be to her buying a new coffee pot?*

"Wow! For me?"

She nodded, and relaxed.

He laughed. "Have you christened it?"

"I bought it Saturday, but I've been too busy with customers to wash it. Beth told me you enjoy your coffee."

He glanced at his shoes and up at her again, then grinned. "What else did she tell you?"

"She told me not to tell you. Do you take your coffee black?"

Joanna dried the pot, her hands trembling, and struggled with the can opener and the coffee can.

How can I be so aware of someone standing at least five feet away?

"Honey, I like coffee any way you can fix it, except instant."

He dropped in the familiar expression so effortlessly that it didn't register to either of them at first. Then he turned red. "I'm sorry. I didn't mean to patronize you." He took the can opener from her, and his hands folded over hers for a second, making her flush warm. "Let me help."

As the seal on the can was penetrated, they raised their chins simultaneously to savor the coffee aroma. Spontaneous laughter cleared the air.

Joanna still felt jittery as she opened a tin of cookies and arranged a few on a plate. "Beth may start making some pastries for me," she said.

He took off his windbreaker and draped it over the back of a chair at the table nearest the counter, then sat down.

Her heart raced. He obviously intended to stay for a while. "I thought you might be closed," he said. "Don't make coffee just for me if you're about to leave."

She had already plugged in the pot, and they could hear the water heating. "I need to know if it works," she said. "Let me turn down the stereo."

"Don't. I love that concerto. That is a harpsichord, isn't it?"

"Bach's *Harpsichord Concerto in F Minor*. You know a lot about music," she said. "Do you play an instrument?"

He laughed. "No. I'm all thumbs. I knew this music was a concerto, and I thought it was a harpsichord, but I don't know all that major and minor stuff. I just love music – but hearing it live is a special gift." He looked at her with a frankness that unnerved her, but Joanna felt a flush of pleasure.

She concentrated on the fact that he and Beth looked very much alike, although he had a more rugged look of the outdoors. She touched her hair with both hands and tucked a wisp into the twist.

"Beth told me about the catering," he said. "That's why we went back to Winston over the weekend. She needed her baking equipment and the rest of her clothes. I think you get the credit for her decision, so thank you."

"You mean she didn't want to stay here?"

"She didn't want to leave the city – but I knew she and Benjie were in danger, and I couldn't take them with me to England." His forehead creased with concern. "I was worried sick about her."

"Danger? England?"

"Oh, Joanna Jerome, that's a long story."

She had not meant to pry. *Are my cheeks pink?*

"I'll tell you all about it sometime," he said. "I promise."

He smiled but not quickly enough to cover the sadness in his expression. This evening the tiny lines in his face appeared deeply etched. He looked weary. His eyes were deep and dark as antique mahogany. Joanna wanted to walk around the table to stroke those lines, soothing some of the fatigue.

She ignored the delicate porcelain cups she reserved for tea, selecting a pottery mug she had bought for her father. Ben didn't seem the type to enjoy a pink rose-covered Royal Doulton cup.

"Beth was right," she said. "My cookies are terrible."

"She said that?"

Joanna put her favorite cup on the table and checked the napkins. "Your nephew is adorable."

Joy spread across his face. "He is! And his mother is one handful."

The coffee pot was gurgling. Joanna stood up.

"Please . . . let me," Ben said. "I'm responsible for your buying the pot and working overtime." He poured their coffee and returned the coffee pot to the counter.

"How's school?" Joanna asked.

"It's different – but I think I'll enjoy the challenge. It's been a couple of years since I taught on the high-school level. I went back to graduate school, and I suppose I've been a university student too long." He paused to study her again. "On the other hand, I know almost nothing about you, Joanna Jerome. Mr. Hughes said you taught organ at the university and that you're an expert on Handel's contemporaries. I guess Bach would be one. I never knew organists had specialties like that."

"I was an accompanist for the music department. I'm not an expert on Handel, but his music – and that of other composers of his time – fascinates me. Let me guess. The next question will be . . ." She looked up at the ceiling. "Why are you holing up in this hick town?"

He groaned. "I knew my sister would embarrass me."

Joanna put a hand on his arm. "No, I wasn't offended."

He seemed grateful that she understood. "She's had a horrible life. I'll tell you about that sometime too." He nodded. "Yep, we have a lot to talk about." He waited for her to continue.

"I came back to Galax Falls to care for my father when he got sick."

Late-afternoon shadows embraced the shop, but they lingered. She refilled their cups. Most of their conversation was trivial, but it gave Joanna a three-dimensional portrait of him. Often they paused to listen to the music.

"What is your pendant? Some music award, I'll bet." He lifted the gold chain and cradled the medallion in his hand.

She leaned toward him. "The Golden Chord Award from my university music sorority. A long time ago."

"It hasn't been so long ago! I've noticed you always wear it – as a connection with the dream, perhaps?"

She caught her breath. *How did he know?*

"But, Joanna Jerome, it's in your future also. Don't look so blue. Great Scott!" he exclaimed. "It's late, and you've got to get home to your dad." He reached into his pocket and pulled out a yellow legal sheet that had been folded carefully.

"My buddy in Winston-Salem who deals in old books came up with this partial price list. There are two or three that he wants to research. He's prepared to offer you the top price right now. You'll have to wait a while if I'm going to buy them."

"Ben, I appreciate your going to all this trouble. I'm in no hurry to sell them. I'll pack them away for you – or you can take them and pay later if you like."

Sadness played around his eyes but did not stay. "You really mean that, don't you? It might be a long, long time before I can come up with extra cash. I think it's best to leave them all here for now, if you don't mind. If you have some boxes, let me pack them for you."

"Okay. I'll call my father and tell him I'll be a bit longer. The boxes are in the back. I'll gladly let your friend buy the others. I need the space."

By the time Joanna got off the phone, he had already pulled out most of the books and carefully dusted them. He knelt beside the counter and placed those he intended to buy in one box, the others in a larger one. He straightened up, smiling. "Did you notice that this copy has a handwritten note from one of the translators?" he asked. "Apparently explaining their interpretation of a word. It's the Lang, Leaf and Myers translation of *The Iliad*. This could be worth a fortune!"

A wistfulness brushed across his brow when he picked up Charlotte Brontë's *Jane Eyre* and laid it in the smaller container. He held a copy of Milton's poems in his hands, protecting it as though he held a fragile flower. "I was to visit John Milton's home this fall."

"I always wanted to do graduate study in England. What were you going to do?" she asked, sitting on the floor beside him, intimacy wrapping around her as comfortably as a favorite sweater.

"I was awarded a full doctoral fellowship. As it turned out, I couldn't accept it." He shrugged as if it didn't matter, but she realized he had given up a great deal to come to Galax Falls.

I know a little about broken dreams, she thought.

His attention was elsewhere, and she leaned sideways to see what had grabbed his interest. "Hey, what's this?" he asked. "Did you know this was here?"

"What is it?"

He pulled a faded gray cardboard folder from behind the books. It was secured with a brown string that once might have been white. Dust rose from it as he carefully untied the string and opened the folder. "I guess it's okay for me to do this," he said.

"Please, go ahead. It's so dusty, I'd be sneezing my head off if I fooled with it."

"Looks like a manuscript."

The yellowed pages looked like translucent parchment paper, as delicate as butterfly wings. His voice sounded breathless as he read aloud, *"A Lackluster Lover* by William Sydney Porter."

"O. Henry," she whispered. "Do you think it's genuine?"

"I don't know. Could be. He grew up in Greensboro. One of the greatest short-story writers of the twentieth century. This could be nearly a hundred years old!"

"The former owner of this shop was a Mr. Henry. He came from Greensboro!"

Cautiously Ben shifted the folder to get a better view. "I won't touch the pages. The oil from my fingers might mark them. See how it's flaking? Looks like it might disintegrate if I breathe on it."

"What should I do with it?"

"Are you sure it's legally yours?" he asked quietly.

"I signed a contract for everything left in the shop. Mr. Henry told me he had left me a surprise in here, if I could find it. I suspected that he had tucked away a piece of jewelry or something like that. He was an old family friend, deeply indebted to my father for some legal transactions. Dad dismissed his debts – and he died soon after he moved away."

"This might be very valuable, Joanna."

"I suspect it is."

"Better put it in a safety deposit box. First, though, why don't you have it photocopied? Print me a copy, and I'll see if my friend in Winston can research it. Isn't it interesting that he wrote under the pen name of O. Henry and you acquired it from a Mr. Henry?"

She gave him a quizzical look. "I'll copy it at Dad's office tomorrow – but tonight I'll take it to show to him. I have a safe place in the back room that will be adequate, at least temporarily." She studied the manuscript, spellbound by curiosity and fascinated by the handwriting that sprawled across the pages like intricate black needlework. The pages smelled like a damp forest.

Ben carried the boxes of books to the back room and stacked them neatly in the closet.

Then he paused to take one more sip from his coffee mug. "I taught a course on Porter at the university several years ago, and there's one fact I always remember about him. He bragged about his feet. Claimed he had freckles on them."

"What a strange thing for you to remember."

"I guess I have a gift for remembering strange things – not as special as a gift for music, but we take what we get. I read several biographies of Porter. He was a small, shy, freckled kid and I guess he used humor to handle his aversion to freckles. He was always considered 'different'." Ben picked up his jacket. "Beth used to be so ashamed of her freckles. I tried to convince her they were cute. When I told her about Porter's feet, she immediately jerked off her shoes to check her own. Promise me, Joanna, that you won't let my sister drive you crazy. Can I help you lock up?"

She waved him away. "You need to check on Beth and Benjie." With trembling fingers she wrapped the manuscript in packing newsprint, then closed up the shop.

The drive home caught her humming. Ben was not a dream. He had moved to Galax Falls, and he had come back into the shop to see her.

"Hearing the music live is a special gift," he had said, "We have lots to talk about."

"Dad," she asked at dinner, after they exhausted the subject of the manuscript and its possible value, "how long did it take for you to fall in love with Mother?"

He laid down his fork and looked pensive, as though remembering something special.

"Oh, honey . . . it took a long time. Almost two full minutes."

She laughed. He didn't – but he reached over to pat her hand.

♫

Chapter Seven

Pungent aromas of yeast and cinnamon permeated the little shop on Thursday morning when Joanna had scheduled an impromptu tasting party. When she saw her dad's part-time housekeeper pull up, she hurried to hold the door for her father.

"Ah!" Nicholas Jerome paused to fill his lungs, then shoved his walker forward. "A virtual bouquet to seduce the olfactory senses."

Beth, standing behind the counter, shot Joanna a worried glance and pushed a strand of hair behind her ear – a mannerism that seemed frequent for her.

"Dad," Joanna said, laughing, "it's your favorite soul food, and the rolls are still warm."

"Terrific." He smiled and twisted around to look at his driver. "Mrs. Campbell, park the car and come in here. You'll not believe the fragrance. Makes my toes tingle."

When he arrived at the counter, he leaned across and extended his hand to the young woman standing behind it. "This must be the talented and witty Beth Morgan! You have already added considerably to the well-being of Galax Falls, my dear."

Beth blushed with joy, and for a moment she looked like an eight-year-old on Christmas morning.

Joanna said, "This is my dad, Nicholas Jerome – and that's our friend Nora Campbell out front."

"Where's the boy?" Mr. Jerome asked.

Benjie stuck his head from the side of the counter and peered up, his eyes huge brown orbs of curiosity. He stared at the walker and pulled back with apprehension.

"Hello there, young man."

Benjie retreated to his mother with a slight whimper, and Mr. Jerome withdrew, clearly surprised by the rebuff.

Beth placed a protective arm around her son. Sadness settled around her eyes. "I think it's the walker. My father uses a wheelchair, and he . . . he frightens Benjie."

Mr. Jerome eased himself into a chair and shoved the contraption aside, Benjie – the same child who had latched onto Ed's leg – was afraid of him. "Son," he said gently, "how's your mother's baking this morning? Come in, Mrs. Campbell, and meet Beth and Benjie." His tone was amicable, but Joanna could tell he was hurt. "Give us a sample, Jo – and something great for Benjie too." He pulled another chair close to him. "Here, lad, you can sit with old Nicholas when you're ready."

Benjie ignored the man. He stared at the aluminum walker.

Mr. Jerome reached for it and moved it away from his own legs but slightly in front of the child. "Want to try it out? We seem to walk with about the same speed and skill." Then, he turned his attention to the table.

Benjie watched with solemn interest.The child positioned himself in front of the walker and stretched to touch the handles. He studied the silver-colored finish and played with the black-plastic hand grips as though he were riding a motorcycle.

"Go!" he demanded.

Everyone laughed. Benjie looked distracted for a split second, then laughed too. Mr. Jerome did not attempt to engage him further.

Joanna put dessert plates in front of her dad and Mrs. Campbell. "Try this," she said.

"Mmm-mm!" her father exclaimed. "You're right, Beth. You'll put this shop on the map with your pastries. Mrs. Campbell, I think you have some competition with your baking."

"No competition," Mrs. Campbell responded politely. "Mrs. Morgan is the clear winner. I would love to have your recipe."

Beth was radiant.

Joanna had not invited Ed Westmoreland to the party, so she knew her father was the catalyst when Ed entered the shop. He glanced around, spotted Beth behind the counter, and hesitated.

Beth blurted, "Hello, Mister Ed."

The lawyer's dignity absorbed the shock. Startled, he glanced at Nicholas when the old man chortled. Mrs. Campbell snickered.

Ed jammed his lips together and pondered. His shoulders relaxed, and to Joanna's amazement, he smiled.

"Beats Dumbo," he said. "That's what they called me, as I was growing up. A talking horse is a little better, I guess." He adjusted his glasses with his middle finger as his eyes skirted around the room. He chose the chair farthest from Benjie.

"Did you get a whiff of the rolls as you walked over?" Nicholas asked.

Ed nodded. "I did, and I nearly ran the rest of the way. I didn't eat breakfast."

Joanna smiled at the image of Ed running, and filled a mug for him. Beth served him a blueberry muffin.

"Out of oats?" he asked in an awkward attempt at humor. He was rewarded with a murmur of subdued laughter, and for several seconds the only sounds in the shop came from the scraping of forks against the plates.

"I'd like to formulate a proposition." Ed spoke up with a garrulous zeal Joanna had never seen in him. "Why don't you put up a sign on the counter advertising your pastries and cooking? I'd be glad to print you some on my computer. Call me and tell me exactly what you want them to say." When he realized that everyone was staring at him, he looked down at his mug, face flushed. He patted his lips with his napkin and studied the tablecloth.

A teasing grin faded from Beth's face, and a sarcastic remark died on her lips. The mischievous look drained away and left a wistfulness that started in her eyes and spread across her face. "Mr. Westmoreland . . ."

"Mister Ed," he returned.

"Ed," she said, smiling. "That would be great, if Joanna doesn't mind. Thanks!" She beamed at him and spoke with such enthusiasm that Ed squirmed.

He shrugged. "No big deal."

"Oh, but it is, to me."

"Fantastic." He fidgeted with his fork.

Nicholas caught Joanna's eye and winked.

Joanna noticed how often Ed stole shy glances

at Beth. He seemed to watch her with dazed disbelief.

Ed quickly finished his dessert and fumbled with his wallet, but Nicholas waved his money away. "It's my party, Ed. Just reach under that counter and hand me that little tin frog. I'll need the key too . . . and sit back down and pay attention for a minute. You can't be that rushed to go back to work. In fact, your boss is insisting that you stay."

"Guess I can't argue then." He grinned.

The frog was a small toy, less than three inches long, cheaply made in Japan in the early thirties. Nicholas nestled it gently in his cupped hand, then covered it with his other hand. Four puzzled adults watched as he spoke to his fist. "Well, hi, Kermit. Feeling lonely all locked up in the dark?"

Benjie watched motionless, his eyebrows arched in bewilderment.

Nicholas spoke quietly, in a soothing tone. "We won't hurt you. Benjie is here, and he wants to pet you. He's a little bit afraid, but I'll assure him that you won't hurt him."

Fascinated, the little boy eased closer, his suspicious look dissipating.

Nicholas continued, making no effort to rush the boy. Joanna realized he was projecting the same unhurried tone he had used with skeptical juries to win difficult cases.

Benjie edged toward Nicholas, breathing heavily. The tip of his tongue moistened the corner of his mouth. He leaned forward. Nicholas seemed to all but ignore the child as he expanded his conversation with the green frog.

"Yes, Kermit, we'll save you some rolls. Benjie's mother is a terrific baker."

Finally Benjie slumped against Nicholas' leg,

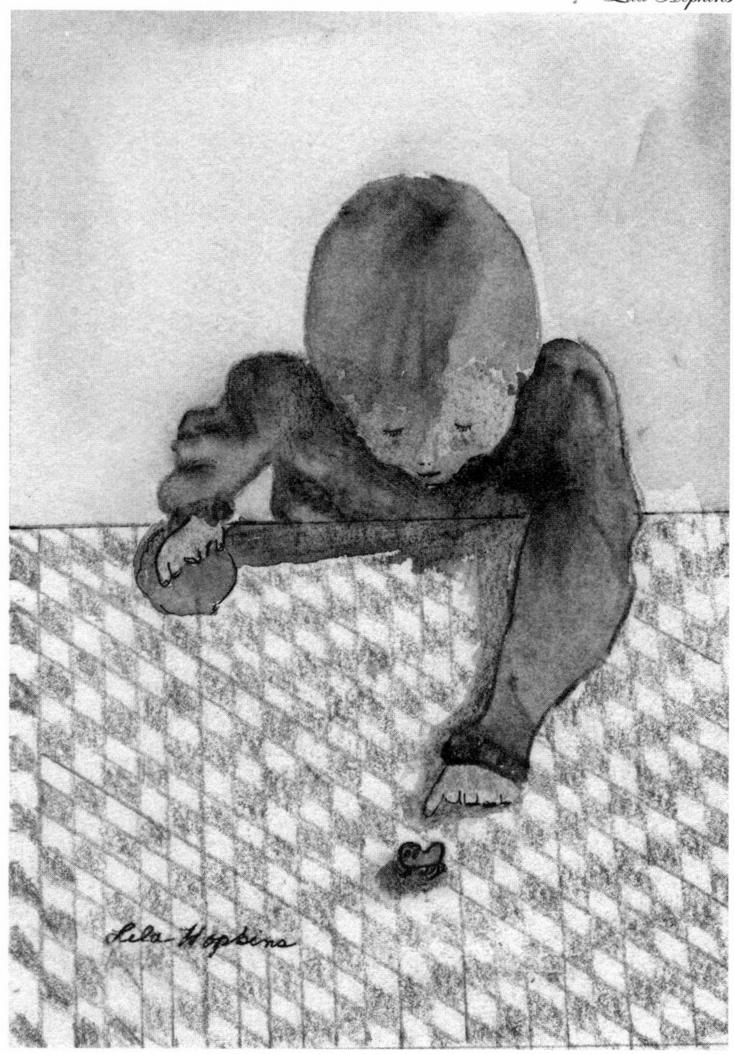

preoccupied by the frog. Nicholas lowered his hand and opened it slightly so the child could study the toy. "Want to pet it?"

Benjie stretched out one finger, then drew back. He sought his mother's reassurance.

Beth smiled, wonder etched in her face.

Nicholas lifted his right hand so Benjie could see the frog better, and the child almost touched it before retreating.

"I can make him hop if you're not afraid of him."

With extreme caution Benjie thrust one trembling finger to the head of the tin toy. He giggled.

The group watched, transfixed, as Benjie pulled himself into the chair next to Nicholas. The old man, his white hair only inches from the blond child, transferred the frog gently from his hand to the little boy's. Benjie concentrated on the toy.

"See this little key? We can use it to wind Kermit up and let him jump across the table."

Benjie turned to Nicholas and extended the toy. "Go."

Nicholas took the frog, and the adults at the table seemed as mesmerized by the clicking sound of the key as the child.

The old man placed the frog on the table. "It's going to rattle and make a noise as it jumps. Ready?"

Benjie nodded.

Nicholas released the frog, and Benjie squealed with delight as the toy leaped across the table, wobbled, made a quick turn, and bounded back.

Joanna stood back against the counter to watch her father and Benjie. Nicholas demonstrated an obvious ease and skill with the child that contrasted with the mystified expression Ed wore. He looked pained. He glanced at Beth.

Nicholas appeared oblivious to the interaction between Beth and Ed, but Joanna knew better. Her father had set Ed up, and she wondered if it was prudent. Still, she trusted him and knew he would do nothing to hurt either his partner or Ben's sister, at least not intentionally.

Moments later, when customers arrived, Joanna saw Ed slip unobtrusively from the shop. Beth gazed thoughtfully after him.

"I hope I didn't offend him," she said in a small voice.

"No," Nicholas responded. "You overwhelmed him."

"That's not good, is it?"

"It's great. Perhaps you can help him unbend a bit. Ed takes life too seriously."

Beth began to clear the table. "Do you have grandchildren, Mr. Jerome?"

"My son lives in Atlanta. His daughters are in high school. I don't have a grandson."

"You ought to have a dozen grandchildren."

"I agree." Nicholas laughed, sounding more pleased than he had in months.

Beth confessed sadly, "My dad hates kids. He scares Benjie to death."

Joanna felt a lump in her throat. Ben said Beth had suffered a horrible life. She looked at her father and realized how lucky she was.

♫

Chapter Eight

Beth parked the stroller on the edge of the wide sidewalk, set the brake, and picked up her son. She looked up at the gray Victorian house and its wide verandah. A sign on the railing said:

Nicholas Jerome
Edward Westmoreland
Attorneys at Law

She rubbed her hand down the leg of her blue jeans. For a moment she considered putting Benjie back into his stroller and leaving. Instead she grabbed the strap of her purse and slung it over her shoulder. Leading with her chin, she strode up the eight steps to the entrance and stepped into the air-conditioned building. Instinctively she pulled Benjie closer.

"Wow!" She took a deep breath. She had expected to hear sounds of a busy office: clicking computers and ringing phones. She entered the hushed reception room, feeling as out of place as a stray cat in Bloomingdale's.

An efficient-looking secretary gave her a long

professional appraisal, and Beth swallowed, knowing she was not dressed for this fancy place. Her feet sank into plush carpet as she timidly crossed the reception room to the desk.

"May I help you?"

Beth swallowed. "Is Ed – Mr. Westmoreland – in – available?"

"Do you have an appointment?"

Beth looked at Benjie and brushed his hair back from his face. "No. He just said to drop by."

"Your name, please?"

She was so flustered that she was not sure she could remember her name right then, but she was spared embarrassment when a door opened and Ed stepped out. He seemed seven feet tall to her.

"It's Mrs. Morgan, Estelle. Come on in, please."

He gave Beth a curt nod, and she preceded him into his office. She felt like a grade-school student being summoned by the principal.

"Whew," she said. "I hope I never need a lawyer up here."

Ed looked startled. "Why do you say that?"

"Ex-pen-sive! Wow! You must be rich."

"Not exactly." He sounded annoyed. "You don't come to Galax Falls to get rich."

"Why did you come? To save the downtrodden? Free the falsely accused?"

Ed stepped backward. He pushed his glasses up on his nose with his middle finger. He stood gaping at her with his mouth half open, speechless.

"You've sure got a lot of art," Beth said. "You know all these artists personally?"

She gazed at the framed pictures, then slid Benjie down into a leather chair and faced Ed.

"Uh . . . have a seat, Beth."

He moved around his desk, picked up a folder, and handed it to her. She looked puzzled as she sank down into the luxurious chair and opened the folder.

"Hey! Neat! You didn't do this by yourself on your computer, did you? Look at this, Benjie. Ed made us some fine advertising posters."

Ed coughed. He adjusted his tie. "Well, actually, I did print them myself."

"Oh, Ed . . . " Emotion caught in her throat.

He looked anxious as Beth stood, fumbled in her jeans pocket, and pulled out a tissue.

"Don't worry." She sat back down. "You're getting nervous, because you think I'm going to cry."

She wiped her nose and sighed. "Well, I feel like it, but I'm not going to start blubbering. This is one of the nicest things anyone has ever done for me." She gazed at him with wide, serious eyes. "I don't intend to let my brother support Benjie and me the rest of my life."

Ed nodded solemnly.

"I was only teasing when I called you Mister Ed. You must be a wonderful man, and I'll bet a very smart lawyer."

He made an odd little sound in his throat. "Aw, no, actually I'm not that smart."

His gaze dropped to his desk, and he played with his pen. He squirmed uncomfortably.

"You made four, five . . . six copies . . . and they look so professional! Look, Benjie. We can put up posters all over town and get us a real catering business started."

Benjie was not impressed. He scrambled down from his chair and lurched toward the desk, pointing, jabbering. Beth followed his gaze and noticed what her son had spotted – a row of ceramic owls ranged across Ed's desk.

"You collect owls." She shifted in her seat so she could look at the walls again. Owls also decorated the bookshelves. "I didn't realize that most of your pictures contain owls. Owls are my favorite bird too," she said. "They don't really twist their heads all the way around. Did you know that? I used to think they would wring their own heads off . . . well, of course you knew that." Her enthusiasm wound down, and she was embarrassed. She looked down at her lap, and her cheeks felt warm. A strand of hair fell across her face, and she brushed it back over her ear.

"There's an awful lot about owls I don't know," Ed said. "I think it's because they can turn their heads with such lightning speed that some people think they can twist their heads off."

She had not expected him to be so kind or wise. "One came down our chimney once," she said hurriedly. "A little fluffy owl." She formed a small ball with her hands. "About this big."

"Was it gray, with little tufts on its head? About six inches long?"

She nodded.

"Probably an eastern screech owl. They have a quavering wail."

"My dad wanted to kill it, but I caught it. Threw a towel over it, and freed it out in the woods."

Ed beamed at her. He positioned his elbows on his desk and leaned across it toward her. "Good for you."

"That's a funny hobby for a man, isn't it? I thought only little old women collected owls."

"Funny? I guess it's hilarious, actually." His voice held no humor. "I've worn thick glasses since I was eight months old. I've always resembled an owl."

Beth was aghast. "That's terrible! You poor thing. That's cruel. Who said you looked like an owl?"

"My brother still calls me Owl."

"And Dumbo?"

He chuckled, and his face was transformed. He had a shy, engaging smile. "And Dumbo. And Mister Ed."

He laughed. Beth had not heard him laugh before.

"I'm so ashamed," she said. "I shouldn't have said that. I don't know what gets into me. I just rattle on sometimes, making no sense at all. You just seemed so *pompous*." Confounded, she slapped her face with both hands and gave him a frightened look. "See what I mean? I'm sorry. I'm just a scatterbrain." She reached around the chair, clutching the folder and frantically groping for her purse. "I know you're very busy. We have to go, Benjie."

She jumped up, and Ed came to his feet slowly.

"I'm glad you like the posters," he said. "They didn't take much time."

He seemed reluctant to see her leave. "If you need more, I can print them easily . . . but I'd like to advise you about something."

"Wait," she said, frowning and holding up a hand. "Is this gonna cost me?"

His eyebrows rose in horror, making him look even more owlish. His Adam's apple bobbed up and down. "You made me forget what I was going to say."

She grinned and grabbed Benjie's hand. "Don't touch Ed's owls, sweetie." She curtsied to

Ed. "It's been an interesting visit, Mr. Attorney."

"Yes, it has," he replied soberly.

She walked to the door before he spoke again. "I remember what I was going to say."

She turned to face him.

"Beth, you don't need to be ashamed. About anything."

She cocked her head and studied him. "Thanks," she said simply, then led Benjie out of the office.

Ed stood at his desk, staring after her.

♫

Chapter Nine

With the final chord of the anthem Joanna knew that the choir, and the organist, had delivered music to rival a celestial chorale. A warm glow spread through her, and as she moved to the chair next to the organ, she sought out her father. She was rewarded with a salute. It was one of the little rituals they practiced, and it always gave her a special pleasure.

After the service Nicholas would wait at the front of the sanctuary to tell her eagerly, "The music was exquisite."

She had to admit, it often was. She worked hard to make it so, but today the performance had a special quality. Ben sang with the choir.

She tried to concentrate on the pastor's sermon, but her thoughts strayed too much. She was relieved when the service was over and she could begin the closing hymn. She could tell from the diminishing sounds that the church was emptying quickly, and she shortened the postlude.

"That was flawless," Ben said behind her.

She had not realized he was there.

He moved to stand beside the organ.

"Not quite," she said, "but I won't point out the errors."

He had a mischievous glint in his eyes. "What's a lady whose music is enough to make the angels cry – "

"That bad?"

"That great. Why's she holing up in a town like this?"

"Making the angels cry." She giggled, an inappropriate response from a dignified church organist.

Ben leaned toward her, and his voice was conspiratorial. "The weatherman says it will be raining all day."

Her voice was weighted by resignation. "So I heard." She turned off the organ and reached for her high-heeled shoes as he waited.

"How about a walk in the rain this afternoon?" he asked.

Her voice vaulted with enthusiasm. "Yes – I'd like that."

"I'll pick you up at two." He leaned across to turn off the light above the music rack.

"Wait, Ben." She touched his arm. "Come meet my dad."

Ben waved at the man standing with the walker. "We've been talking," he said. "He seems to know the church organist. He told me how to find her house."

"I should have known." She faced her father and shook her head to scold him. He shrugged, projecting an exaggerated image of innocence.

♫ ♫ ♫

Joanna changed to lightweight slacks and dug an old green windbreaker out of her closet. She found a Western-style hat she had been given when she played a concert in Santa Fe and plopped it on her head, excited about spending some time with Ben.

She studied her reflection in the mirror, and a hint of fear flickered in her. She didn't want to set herself up for heartbreak. *Please, dear God, don't let me make a fool of myself. It would be very easy for me to fall in love with Ben.*

He arrived wearing short sleeves, blue jeans, hiking boots, and an adventurous grin. When they were in his car, he asked, "Do you have a favorite place to hike?"

"Oh, yes. There are lots of fine trails on the Parkway, and my favorite is Rough Ridge, but it will likely be too slippery and dangerous in the rain."

"We'll save it until next time. I've never had a chance to explore Bobcat Lake. Would that be too elementary for you? I'm kinda rusty. Some day soon, I'd like to climb to the top of the falls."

She was relieved, because she too had neglected her love of hiking in recent years. "I'd love that . . . Don't you need a jacket?" she asked after he parked and opened her door.

"Naw. I love to walk with the wind and rain in my face and on my arms. Makes me feel invincible!" He squared his shoulders, stuck his hands into his pockets, and marched into the rain. She followed, laughing.

♫ ♫ ♫

Ozone spiced the air, and the dampness accentuated the pungent fragrance of evergreens. Joanna raised her face toward the sky, and the gentle rain fell silky and cool on her face. Ben led the way across the parking lot until they reached the woods. "It's slippery on these wet leaves. Take my hand."

The quiet woods, with only sounds of dripping water from the trees, projected a sense of solitude. Already they seemed miles from civilization.

He was in much better physical shape than

she anticipated, and soon she was breathless.

"Hey, stop a minute! I can't keep up."

"I'm sorry." He slowed and soon she got her second wind.

Dense fog, rising from the nearby lake, clothed the familiar trail in an exotic sense of adventure. They walked in silence for almost half an hour. Sometimes he had to drop her hand and let her go ahead of him on the narrow path, but each time the passage broadened, he took her hand again. They did not see any animals, not even a squirrel. No bird call marked cadence for their hike. All of nature seemed eerily still.

They brushed by lacy, fernlike hemlocks in the mist. Rhododendrons appeared, fat flower buds already formed, waiting for spring.

The majestic Blue Ridge Mountains encompassed them, obscured by rain and clouds. She sensed their presence, like old friends, circling the lake, isolating it from the rest of the world. Joanna could have described every lofty peak that towered above Galax Falls.

How much do I know about this man? His concern for her safety on the path and the way he shielded her from overhanging branches showed his caring. His commitment to care for Beth and Benjie gave her a strong faith in his integrity. His love of music gave her a special, priceless kinship with him. She made up her mind to show him the grandeur of the Blue Ridge.

They scaled a steep hill, and both were breathing heavily, when they came to a picnic shelter. Ben climbed onto the table, using the bench as a footstool, and extended his hand to help her up.

"Less wind up here," he said, "and we can dry off a little."

Joanna removed her hat and shook out her dark hair. "Your hair looks so pretty down around your face," he said quietly. He brushed some water from her cheek, and she was acutely aware of his gentle touch.

"You promised to tell me what rain dust is," she said.

"Rain dust? I read that in a poem once. It's the promise of the rainbow pot of gold, or the mystique of happiness ever after. It's produced by long walks in the rain and a man getting his life in perspective with a beautiful woman like you."

"Sure. Rain frizzes my hair and smudges my makeup."

"Makeup? You?" He laughed. "I thought you were a totally natural girl." His face relaxed, and a playful smile danced around his mouth. "I *knew* you liked to walk in the rain," he said. "We'll have to get into training, and I'll have to find a felt hat. Yours certainly turns the water."

"I've spent a lot of time hiking. Nature was always my father's love – almost as much as music was my mother's. I guess I inherited both . . . "

"What would you study in Europe?" he asked.

"More work with the harpsichord."

"Do you mean to tell me that there is more about music that you actually want to study?"

"My work was just beginning when . . . "

"I know. Where's your dream medallion?"

"I didn't need it today." She marveled that he was so perceptive.

He changed the subject then. "I know you don't want to *marry* Ed." He paused to smile at her, and they both recalled the scene in the shop when Ben overheard their conversation. "But what *do* you think of him?" he asked. "Beth seems taken with him."

"He's my father's partner, and Dad has the highest opinion of him. The chemistry just wasn't right for us. He's honest and trustworthy but too pontifical for me, so rigid and unbending. Except for Dad, we didn't have much in common. He doesn't care much for music, and it's my life. I can't imagine being married to him."

Ben nodded thoughtfully. "I don't want Beth hurt again," he said. "He's much older than she is and the opposite of her ex-husband."

"Perhaps that's his appeal."

He looked at her, his eyes clouded by misgivings. "But what could he see in Beth?"

"Hey! You're not being fair to Beth. He'll protect her, take care of her. She brings out the best in him. You shouldn't underestimate her, Ben."

"But Benjie . . ."

She dropped her gaze, thinking that Benjie might present a problem, then recalling her father's wisdom. "You know, Dad seems to think that Benjie will take care of that. He says Ed's afraid of children because he's never been around them. He thinks Beth is just what Ed needs. Did she tell you about her first encounter with him at the shop?"

"I'd like to hear you tell it."

She almost laughed but checked herself. It might not be funny to Ben. She tried to remember every phrase Beth used, every expression on Ed's face, and finally could not hold her mirth in check as she described Ed's consternation when Benjie grabbed his leg. She told how Ed's back stiffened and about his gallop to the door when Beth called him a "handsome devil."

Ben joined in her laughter, then sobered. "But

that wasn't Beth! She was trying to play the comedian. But inside she's a lonely, scared little girl seeking love and security."

"How do you know that Ed can't give her that?"

"Perhaps . . . we don't even know if he's interested in her. He offers to print her some promotional posters, and she goes nuts." He sighed and paused a moment. "He doesn't strike me as the fatherly type," he said, "and Benjie is part of the package. I see Ed with a tall, sophisticated woman on his arm, going to an expensive restaurant where he can snap his fingers and get the best table in the house."

"I dated him for months, and he never took me to an expensive restaurant. And I never saw him snap his fingers for a table."

"Really? How many McDonald's did you visit with him?"

"McDonald's? Ed Westmoreland?"

"Exactly. See what I mean? McDonald's is Beth's speed."

He's right. They were silent again. Joanna noticed that the rain was tapering off, but she was in no hurry to end this conversation.

Ben glanced at her, then shifted his eyes to the lake, visible in the distance now that the fog was dissipating. "I don't regret assuming responsibility for Beth and Benjie, but it means that I have to put a lot of my own life on hold. I hope you understand."

Is he giving me a gentle warning? Finally Joanna found the courage to ask him. "You have dissected Ed. How do you evaluate me?"

He leaned over to touch her hand. "Well, in the first place, as an English teacher I pay attention to verb tenses, and I'm glad to hear you use the past tense when you speak about dating Ed."

He studied her, his eyes serious and penetrating as though he could interpret her most secret thoughts. He pulled her arm up under his and encased her hand with both of his. As they leaned their shoulders against each other, a serene satisfaction warmed Joanna in spite of the fall chill.

Ben squeezed her hand and stared into space. He spoke as if in a trance and, imitating a fortuneteller, answered her question at last. "I see a confident, unflappable lady who has it all together. I see a beautiful, loving daughter willing to give up a brilliant career to care for her father."

She inhaled deeply. "Has it all together? Me?"

"Don't you? You don't seem to lack anything."

Oh, Ben . . . if you only knew . . .

"Unflappable?" she returned. "That's my cover– just as Beth's brazen personality is hers."

"You are steady and dependable. You project a deep faith and commitment." His voice dropped to a whisper. "You bring me peace."

They sat in the dreary picnic shelter on that gray afternoon, with the nippy rain falling around them. He made no effort to kiss her or offer love or romance, yet suddenly a rainbow danced across Joanna's horizon, giving her promise of a new life – and she knew she was content to wait.

She did not trust herself to paint an appraisal of him, nor did he ask for it.

"Does your dad fish?" he inquired, breaking into her thoughts.

"Used to. He goes out when my brother visits from Atlanta, which isn't often. Andy's a television anchor on CNN."

"Sure! I watch him! So Andy Jerome is your brother. Well, maybe I can take your father fishing some Saturday. I want to get to know him better. He seems to be a prince of a man, and I love spending time with his daughter." He spoke so quietly that she would wonder later if he actually said it.

"My dad *is* a prince, and he misses getting out. He has a nice boat, by the way. Thanks, Ben."

"Hey, look! It's quit raining. Let's go on around the lake." He pulled her to her feet.

♫ ♫ ♫

That night Joanna lay in bed, reliving the afternoon's walk and talk.

What would I have said if Ben asked me what I thought of him? *Would I have had the nerve to answer honestly, "I think you are my dream come true?"*

She smiled to herself. It took almost two minutes to fall in love with Ben. She reminded herself sternly that, for now, she held second place to Beth and Benjie.

"Okay," she said aloud, "I'll wait." What if he had persisted by asking, *"And the chemistry between us?"* She admitted to herself now that the chemistry was just right.

But, *would he fall in love with her? What if, by the lake, he had whispered that he loved her?*

♫

♫

Chapter Ten

Like the haunting refrain of a musical rondo, memories from Sunday's hike circled endlessly through Joanna's brain as though on an old-fashioned record.

"You bring me peace . . . I have to put my life on hold . . . I love spending time with his daughter . . . You bring me peace . . . I have to put my life on hold . . ."

She expected to hear from him again soon, but he did not call or come by to see her on Monday, and she ended up pouring out a fresh pot of coffee she prepared especially for him. He might love spending time with her, but he was not making any effort to see her.

Is he just an elusive infatuation in my life, drifting in and out like an apparition?

Joanna could not accept that kind of attachment. Her growing misgivings about the strange new relationship dominated her thoughts and disturbed her dreams. A sadness enveloped her and she had trouble throwing it off.

Unflappable? Apparently not in matters of the heart.

Sunday night she had told herself that she

would wait forever. Two days later she was yearning for affirmation of his feelings toward her.

Each day's brightest moment came when Beth drove up to the back door with her delivery. Benjie had inherited his mother's effervescence, and his smile could cheer up the most disgruntled of the downhearted.

This morning Beth bubbled with excitement.

"Did you know your dad has 'commissioned' – his word – a dinner party for Saturday night?"

"For Ed's birthday," Joanna said, taking Benjie from his mother's arms.

Beth hurried to the car for a load of pastries and continued chattering before she entered the shop. "I've never been invited to a party I catered before. Do you think it's okay?"

"It's Dad's party, and he can invite whomever he wants, as long as he's paying for it."

"But what about Ed?"

Joanna laughed. "He'll be okay."

"Do you think I should try to find a babysitter? Ben says no."

"You wouldn't dare! I suspect Benjie is the main person Dad really wants to invite."

Beth looked relieved and pleased. "I'm going to bake a beautiful cake. Nicholas said to discuss the menu with you. Do you have a few minutes now?"

♫ ♫ ♫

Late Tuesday Joanna was unpacking a new shipment of English teapots when Ben opened the door. She wanted to be mature enough not to show her hurt, so she bit her lip and raised her eyes to his.

He didn't say a word. He just looked at her. She fidgeted and looked down.

"Aren't these beautiful?" She lifted a porcelain teapot and brushed packing paper from it.

"The entire scene is heart-stopping, Joanna. You're as beautiful as I remembered in every detail of my dreams. You hair, by the way, looks gorgeous, flowing around your shoulders."

"Is that why you stayed away so long?" Her voice sounded sharp, even to her own ears.

He looked shocked. He dropped his arms to his sides. "I have responsibilities that I must honor. I thought I explained that to you." He studied her face, apparently looking for some sign of reassurance.

"I haven't made coffee *today*."

"You mustn't keep coffee for me. My schedule is going to be so chaotic that I won't be able to keep up with it myself. Hey, you keep unpacking. I know my way around in a kitchen – even this shelf you refer to as a kitchen."

She did not respond, and he continued talking as he moved around the counter and opened the coffee tin. "I've lived alone so long that I certainly know how to make coffee." He looked so at home rummaging around in her space, she felt her spirits lifting.

"So, how's it going?" he asked.

She had to smile at the wistfulness in his eyes. "It's good to see you, Ben." Seeing the relief in his face made her feel a little ashamed. "You wouldn't believe the hit Beth has made," she said. "I'm going to have to hire extra help. Her rolls and cakes sell out before noon."

"Well, you might be able to hire all the help you'll ever need. Grip Lineberger called me from Winston today, and he thinks you may have a gold mine in that manuscript. He wants to come up next week to take a look at it."

"If I could hire help in the shop," Joanna responded quietly, "I could do my organ practice during the day and not have to leave Dad alone so much in the evenings."

The smell of the coffee and sound of the coffee maker drew her to come around the counter and stand beside him. She found two mugs, then moved quickly away from him, but he reached for her and drew her into his arms. She yielded herself against him and laid her head close to his shoulder.

The front door opened. Joanna jumped away from him. "Hello, Mrs. McKittrick." She knew that her face was flushed. "The new teapots came! Let me show you."

Ben faded into the background while Joanna performed as shopkeeper. When she had completed the sale and Mrs. McKittrick was gone, she slid into the chair next to him at the table.

"I didn't mean to embarrass you," he said.

She giggled. "It's okay – but why do you make me giggle? Giggling is for adolescents."

He smiled and sipped his coffee. "I have a class in Spruce Pine in two hours."

"Spruce Pine? Ben, you haven't taken on another job, have you?"

"It's just two nights a week." He brushed aside that subject. "I need to ask you a couple of things. Grip wants to know if you'll object to some publicity about the manuscript and books. It could help him negotiate better prices, and since he usually sells on consignment, it could mean a better price for you. So, can he pick up the books he wants next week?"

"I'd be glad for him to come, and I have no objection to the publicity. I assume he'll want to do some tests on the manuscript. I know they usually check the ink and paper to authenticate old papers."

"Why don't you talk it over with Nicholas? There could be a security problem, since the manuscript may be so valuable. Of course, it could be a fake, you know."

"I'm prepared for a fake. Nothing about the manuscript seems real – but, Ben, you should be proud of Beth."

"I am – bless her heart – she's really worried about my extra work, but it's only a one-semester contract. She's certain that she's going to get lots of catering jobs, so I 'don't have to support them' she says."

"Have you seen her today? She's booked for a big dinner party Saturday night. You and Benjie are invited too."

He looked surprised. "A party? Where?"

"Our house. Dad is throwing a birthday party for Ed."

"Sure Ed will want to see me?"

She laughed. "He doesn't know you were hiding behind the counter that eventful day."

"Whew! Don't you ever tell him." Ben drained his mug and set it on the counter. "I've got to go."

"How about calling me tonight? I'll talk to Dad about the publicity."

"It might be very late. I almost forgot. I came to ask for a date. Our first high school football game is this week. Can you go with me?"

Well, that was a start. He wanted to spend time with her.

♫ ♫ ♫

The call finally came and it was late, but Joanna grabbed the phone with relief. At first, everything seemed normal enough. The course, English as a Second Language, was comparatively easy to teach. Good – he was glad Nicholas agreed to Grip's request.

"You sound tired, Ben."

"I'm exhausted – and worried to death. Is there any chance of Nicholas taking new clients?"

"What on earth is wrong?" she asked, alarmed.

Ben took a deep breath. "Thank God, Beth forgot to check the mail, so I went by the post office as I drove into town. She had a suspicious-looking letter – I've become all too familiar with her harassing mail – and I opened it. Her ex-husband's brother is threatening to kidnap Benjie as retaliation for her testimony at the trial."

"Oh, Ben . . . "

"I don't want to involve Ed – and I don't want to scare Beth to death with the police, at least not until I have to bring them into it."

"Dad will help you," Joanna assured him.

"Are you sure he's up to it?" he asked with a catch in his voice.

"I'm sure, Ben. You know how deeply he cares about Benjie."

"Thanks. I'll call him in the morning. Goodnight, honey."

She cradled the phone against her cheek, unwilling to break the connection until he hung up.

♫

♫

Chapter Eleven

It was an odd combination of dinner guests, Joanna noted, including one man who had proposed to her and the one she hoped would.

The table was set with her mother's loveliest paper-thin Wedgwood and crystal. Tonight she missed her mother badly and knew that her father did, because he had acquired her favorite flowers, out-of-season purple and yellow irises, for the centerpiece.

I wish my mother could have known Ben.

Besides ordering the flowers, her dad invited the guests, arranged for the food, and hired Mrs. Campbell for the cleanup detail. The seating placement was up to Joanna. Because the party was to honor Ed, she put him beside her father with Beth on the other side of Nicholas. That left Joanna sitting between Ben and Benjie. She had a slight trepidation about putting Beth directly across from Ed – until she saw Ed's face when he saw her.

Forsaking blue jeans for a glamorous multicolored, ankle-length skirt and pink silk blouse, Beth had lost her waif-like illusion. Her short blonde hair curled around her face, and small rhinestones sparkled at her ears. Her dark blue eyes danced with excitement. When she glided from the kitchen into the living room, where Nicholas was introducing Ed to Ben, Ed audibly caught his breath.

Nicholas radiated pleasure. Joanna knew that her father thought Beth's transformation was a smashing success. *Let the unbending of Ed begin.*

"Come, Benjie," Nicholas said. "Let's lead the procession to the banquet."

Beth eased forward with her son. "We can walk with Mr. Jerome. Okay, Benjie?"

"'Kay," he said, then fell into step beside the walker.

"Ed, I can't seat the lady with this contraption," Nicholas declared. "Will you do the honors?"

Beth located her and Benjie's place cards, then lifted him to his chair and started to pull out her own. She blushed as Ed came to assist her. She flashed him a heart-stopping smile.

"Now, Benjie," the host announced, "we pray."

Benjie placed the palms of his hands together and bowed his head. As Joanna watched him, she felt a lump in her throat. *Could he really be in danger? How could anyone hurt this child – or his mother? Kidnap Benjie?* The thought made her sick at her stomach.

Nicholas prayed. "Our Father, thank You for this feast and this special gathering of friends. Thank You for this, our new family. Please keep us, and all whom we love, safe. Amen."

Beth said timidly, "That was beautiful, Nicholas. You called us a family. That's wonderful."

"Amen," Ben whispered.

"Eat!" Benjie demanded.

"My sentiments exactly," the host said. "Ed, start the stuffed pork chops."

"It smells wonderful," Joanna said, eliciting murmurs of assent.

Joanna observed Beth watching the faces of the men as they sampled her cooking. She seemed to breathe a little easier when she saw the looks of approval.

Nicholas laid down his fork and looked at her. "So tell me, young lady. How did you develop such superb culinary skills?"

"Aw, shoot," she said, lowering her eyes, "anyone who can read can cook."

"Perhaps," Ed said, holding up a feather-light roll, "but not like this!"

Later Nicholas drew Beth into the conversation. "I hear you visited our offices. What do you think of them?"

"Your place is doodlebug dandy!"

Nicholas chuckled.

Ed, however, looked bewildered. "Doodle what?"

"Doodlebug dandy. That's just an expression I made up." Beth thrust her chin forward and added gently, "It's a joke, Ed."

He looked embarrassed and snickered, but it was not robust laughter.

"Ben, did I tell you that Ed collects owls?" Beth asked. "He has more owls in his office than you have ever seen – and I've been meaning to ask you, Mr. Attorney, can owls really see in the dark?"

"We-e-ll-l," Ed said, drawing out the word, "actually, I've never been an owl." He seemed pleased by the laughter that erupted. When it died down, he declared, "They have keen eyesight, but they rely on their hearing to get around in the dark."

"They have *ears*? Where?"

Ed leaned forward, animated with enthusiasm. "On the little screech owl, like the one you rescued from the fireplace, there are little openings in the side of the head, hidden by feathers. On the barn owl the large ear openings are right beneath the rim of the white facial disks."

"Golly! Ed Westmoreland, you are a walking encyclopedia."

His cheeks turned red. "Aw . . . tell them how you caught the owl trapped in your fireplace."

He acts like a different man when he's talking with her, Joanna thought. *She* is *just what he needs.* "Incidentally, Ed," Joanna dabbed at her lips with her napkin to cover a grin. "Cindy brought in some more Little Guys this week. There's an owl you really must see."

"Really? I know they're all a little different, but I think I have one of every one she makes."

"These are new. There's one with glasses. I've been calling him 'Ed the Owl' all week."

"Et tu, Brutessa," Ed sounded pained, but couldn't suppress a grin as he pointed to Beth. "See what you started."

♬ ♬ ♬

Later Ben said, "My friend Grip Lineberger is coming Tuesday to study the manuscript Joanna found. Ed, I assume it's still in your safe."

For several minutes the conversation centered on the books and manuscripts. There was an intense discussion about security along with speculation about the manuscript possibly being genuine.

Beth asked her brother, "What do you think the manuscript might be worth?"

"I have no way of knowing, but I've read about old books going for more than a hundred."

"A hundred dollars? Just for bunch of yellowed old pages?"

"I meant a hundred *thousand*, little sister – and it's far more than a bunch of yellowed pages."

"What? A hundred thousand? *Dollars*?" Her eyes were wide, and her mouth gaped open. "Wow! That would buy *some* house – or castle."

"Not in Blowing Rock, or anywhere around here," Nicholas said.

"Why, I'll bet one of those old books would pay for a second-hand car, so I wouldn't have to borrow Ben's."

Joanna laughed, and Ben chuckled uncomfortably.

Ed spoke up. "Just a minute. Nicholas, I'm worried about the fiduciary responsibilities of our firm."

Nicholas' response was quick. "The client is my daughter."

"Oh, yes. Of course." His face flushed, Ed looked at his plate.

"You forget one thing," Joanna said. "The manuscript might be a fake. I'm going to ask Grip to take it back to Winston-Salem if he thinks it could be genuine. Then none of us will have to worry about it."

Quietly Beth and Joanna began to clear the table. No one had mentioned the reason for the party until Beth entered the dining room with the birthday cake, alight with candles. Joanna quickly rearranged things on the table so she could place it in front of Ed.

He was speechless.

Ben led everyone in a spirited round of "Happy Birthday To You."

When he found his voice, Ed asked quietly, "Nicholas, may I borrow your camera? I want a picture of the magnificent piece of art to keep forever."

Responding to a look from her father, Joanna got the camera.

Benjie wiggled out of his seat and moved around the table until he stood beside Ed. "Me. Me see." He raised his arms to be lifted. Joanna held her breath.

Ed frowned. He hesitated.

"Me see!" Benjie repeated.

Ed gave Benjie a thin smile, shrugged his shoulders and gingerly hoisted the child to his knee, just as Nicholas snapped a picture.

Benjie laughed, posing again for the camera.

Ben came to his feet and walked around the table. "Allow me, Nicholas."

"Please. You are taller. Thank you. Get one as Benjie helps him blow out the candles!"

"Blow out the candles?" Ed asked. "What do you mean?"

Benjie knew, and soon Ed caught on.

As Beth cut the cake, she asked, "Ed, haven't you ever blown out candles on a birthday cake?"

"I've had birthday cakes before but never with candles meant to be blown out. My mother would have thought it was most unsanitary."

"You poor dear. No wonder you act so strange – but that's all right, Ed. We won't tell your mother."

♫ ♫ ♫

They moved to the living room, and at Ben's insistence Joanna opened the baby-grand piano. They gathered around and performed a second, better, rendition of "Happy Birthday."

Benjie climbed up onto the piano bench and

sat beside Joanna, his little legs swinging in time to the music. Occasionally he stroked a key gently, as he watched every move she made.

Nicholas burst into "It's a Grand Night For Singing." An eager group formed around the piano for a songfest. They worked through several favorites: "Blue Moon" and "I've Got You Under My Skin."

Nicolas's voice sounded tired when he requested a hymn. Joanna played an introduction to his favorite and they all sang: "A mighty fortress is our God, a bulwark never failing; our helper He amid the flood . . . "

"One more," Joanna said, finally. She dared not wear her father out. She began a few measures and Ben said, "That's one of my favorites." He began in a beautiful baritone: "I'd rather have Jesus than silver or gold." The others remained silent, listening, "I'd rather be His than have riches untold. I'd rather have Jesus than houses or lands." His eyes never left Joanna as he sang, and when he had finished, the notes seemed to linger, in testimony to his faith.

"Amen," Nicolas whispered and it was the benediction to the sing-a-long.

Suddenly Beth asked, "Where's Benjie?"

Nicholas pointed. Ed was slumped sleepily on the couch. Leaning against him, covered by Ed's coat and sound asleep, was the little boy. Ed opened one eye. "I'm no night owl." He produced a worthy imitation of a snore.

♫ ♫ ♫

Just as the group was breaking up, Nicholas asked, "Did you read about that naturalist who's going to lecture this week at ASU in Boone? His special interest is owls. Ed, I think you ought to go and take Beth with you. She told me that owls are her favorite birds too."

Ed gulped. "Would you like to go, Beth?"

She looked at her brother.

"I don't have classes on Monday or Friday evening. I can babysit either night," Ben said.

Joanna saw a quick exchange of glances between Ben and Nicolas and realized they were remembering the kidnap threat. Beth seemed unalarmed. *Isn't it unfair not to warn her?* Joanna wondered.

"I'll call you," Ed said to Beth, then hurried self-consciously down the steps toward his car.

♫

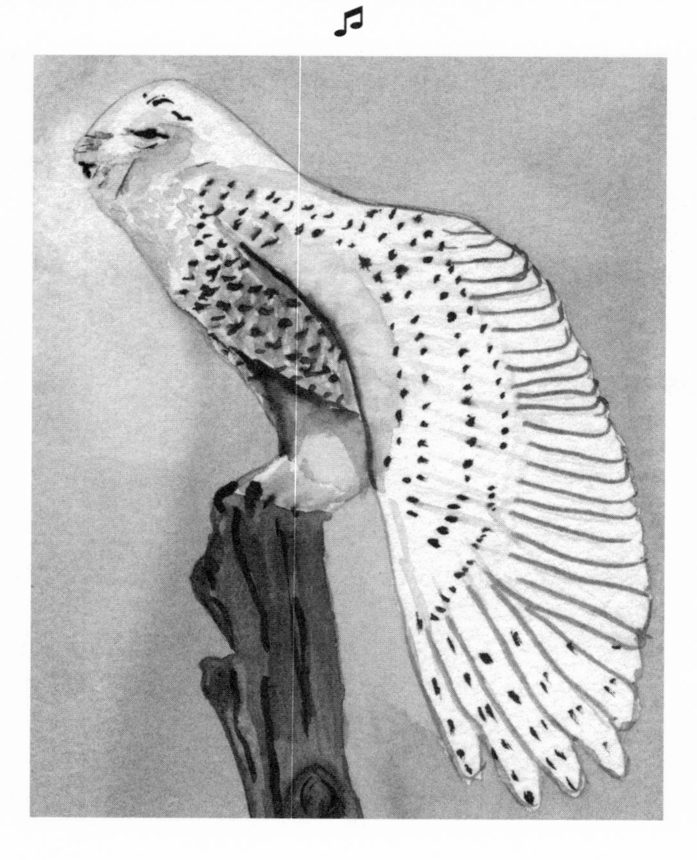

♫

Chapter Twelve

As the sleek black BMW slid through gentle curves of the road toward Boone, on the way to dinner and the lecture, Beth was oblivious to the behind-the-scene activities of Ben and Nicholas.

At that moment Ben was escorting a police officer around their house. The officer was suggesting security procedures and setting up a surveillance plan.

Nicholas had talked with the postal authorities and was seriously considering hiring a bodyguard for Benjie, although the expense seemed prohibitive. He was also spending this evening with a detective.

Knowing nothing about that, Beth took a few minutes to appreciate the luxurious interior of Ed's automobile with its maroon leather upholstery and tinted glass. "Great Scott, Ed, you have everything in here but the kitchen sink."

He chuckled. "I'm pleased that you like it."

She turned to face the dashboard, squashed her shoulders back against the contoured seat, and smoothed down her skirt.

"You can adjust the seat," Ed said, "to make

it more comfortable. Use those little knobs next to the seat."

"I won't touch a thing. Might be an ejection switch!"

They rode in splendid smooth silence for several minutes until she asked, "Since you aren't in your office, may I ask a few questions without getting a bill for your legal services?"

"What could you possibly ask me that you'd expect a bill for?"

"I want a gun permit."

The glossy BMW took a sudden lurch to the right and almost left the highway. Ed grappled with the steering wheel and pulled back up off the shoulder. "A gun permit! What on earth for?"

"To shoot a man, if I have to."

He gulped. "Beth, have you any idea how many accidental shootings there are in this country every year?"

"If I'm aiming the gun, the shooting *won't* be accidental."

"Beth!"

"Look, can you get me one or not?" she asked through clenched teeth. "If not, I'll find another way to buy a weapon."

She crossed and recrossed her arms impatiently.

Ed rubbed his cheek and pushed his glasses back up on his nose. He broke out in a sweat. "I have been successful in getting a few permits," he said. He reached into his jacket pocket, pulled out a handkerchief, and swiped at his forehead.

"What'll it cost, and what do you need to know?"

"Have you talked this over with your brother?"

"No." She could not keep her voice steady, but she prodded on grimly. "Just tell me what kind of information you need, Ed. Birth certificate? Driver's license?"

"I'll have to check the application. I know you can't have a criminal record, and you have to be – "

"Stop right there." She held up her hand. "What kind of criminal record?"

He swerved each time he turned to look at her, his eyes intense with anxiety. "I think the application asks about arrests and police records, which certainly couldn't apply to you. Beth, I wish you would tell me what this is all about. Why would you need a gun permit?"

"Oh, forget it."

"Young lady, I can't forget it," he said sternly, the muscles in his jaw tightening, "but here's our restaurant." He slowed down to make a left turn into the parking lot, but he did not turn off the engine. "You can't ask me to get a gun permit, talk about shooting a man, then just ask me to forget it without an explanation."

Beth unfastened her seatbelt and refused to look at him. "You gonna turn this thing off? It probably has those fancy lights that go off by themselves, but does the engine?"

Ed switched off the ignition key.

"I really don't want an inquisition," Beth said. "I've been getting some threatening calls, but I've been hiding them from Ben." She gripped the armrest. "I won't let anyone take Benjie away from me."

Ed's voice rose in shock. "Take Benjie? Nobody in his right mind would do that – wait a minute. Just a minute! You're receiving threatening telephone calls?"

Ed's professional attention slid smoothly into gear. He assumed his lawyer's demeanor, and Beth took a deep breath. "That's a federal offense," he declared. "I'll call the authorities. We'll get a tracer and a phone block if necessary. We'll put your tormentor in jail."

She looked at him in shock, and whispered, the words packed with emotion, "Oh, Ed . . . "

He looked a little startled.

"You're so powerful and smart!" She dropped her hands into her lap and fidgeted with the pleats in her skirt. Her hair fell across her face. "I can't afford to be your client."

He reached over and clumsily brushed her hair back behind her ear. "Beth, you aren't my client – you're my friend."

"I wish I'd gone right over to your office when I got the first call. I thought about it."

He smiled. "We'll work on it," he said. "Do you want to go into the restaurant? I can take you home if you're too upset."

"Let's eat. Don't get all agitated, Ed. I've been through a lot of this stuff. I know Ben is with Benjie tonight, and he's safe. Let's just have some fun."

When Ed opened the door for her, she stood up, staggered, and stumbled into his arms.

"Oh, my," he said, catching her, "are you all right?" He held her tightly, and for a moment she clung to him like a frightened child. Then she pulled herself together, sniffling loudly and disengaged herself from his embrace.

"Sorry. I tripped."

His palm, braced against her shoulder, felt warm and reassuring as he steered her gently into the restaurant.

"This is a fancy place," Beth whispered as the hostess checked his reservation. She smiled at her handsome escort and brushed a residual tear from her cheek, making a valiant effort to look happy.

"Are you okay?" he asked.

"Yes, thank you. I've never been out with a distinguished lawyer before, and by hokey, I intend to enjoy every minute."

His effort to smile did not disguise the concern in his eyes. Beth felt a growing tenderness toward him.

The rest of the evening seemed unreal. At the restaurant Beth felt like Cinderella, and afterward at the university the lecture was fascinating, with computerized videos of owls from all over the world. Beth noticed with chagrin that for once she was one of the few people in the room *not* in jeans. There was no more talk about gun permits. In fact, the trip home started out in companionable silence.

"What's wrong?" Beth asked, startled when Ed pulled to the shoulder.

"I'm not sure. Must have a flat." He got out of the car, walked around it, and climbed back in. "Guess I do have a flat tire. Right rear. I'll call my service-station mechanic. I'm sorry for the delay." He reached under the seat, pulled out his cell phone, and punched a series of buttons. She listened to the repetitious ring as they waited quietly. "Must be closed," he said finally. "I don't know what to do. I guess I could call my secretary. She'd find someone to help."

Beth stared at him. "Aren't you going to fix it?"

He cringed. "I've never changed a tire before."

"Then I'll do it. I've got to get home."

"You?" His voice was high-pitched and squeaky now. "You will *not*."

"I've changed dozens . . . well, several . . . look, I've changed a tire before. I can do it. Where is your jack manual? We'll need to read it first."

"My what?"

"Your jack manual. I think it's usually with the spare tire."

Ed cleared his throat. "Well, I guess that would be in the trunk . . . but you are not – "

"You'll have to hold the flashlight."

Ed did not stir.

"You do have a flashlight, don't you?"

"Of course – but I'll just walk back to that service station we passed a little while ago and hire some help." He loosened the knot of his tie and slowly pulled it off, then folded it tidily and laid it on the back seat. He reached into the glove compartment for the flashlight.

"Dumb. That's plain dumb. Ed, just push the button and open the trunk. If we can't change it, we can call Ben."

He remained immobile and gave a deep sigh.

"Push the button, Ed."

He pushed it.

They exited their respective doors. Beth watched as he methodically removed his coat, folded it, and laid it across the back seat over the tie. They met at the rear of the car. Ed peered into the lighted interior of the trunk and peeled back the carpet.

They were staring at the tire well when a car passed them, braked, spun around, and came back past them. It made another U-turn before pulling up behind them. Beth raised her hands to shield her eyes from the headlight glare.

Ed said, "Get back into the car and lock it until I see who this is."

"Hey, Mr. Westmoreland!" a friendly voice said, delaying Beth's retreat. "I recognized your car."

A big, burly man joined them, his bulk looming over them in the headlights. "Having trouble? Wait . . . you'll get your clothes dirty. I'll change that tire. I owe you one. Remember when I had to sue my landlord?" To Beth he said, "Young lady, you look like you were expecting an ambush!"

Ed chuckled. "Well, Mr. Haynes! You are a sight for sore eyes. I would be so pleased if you would help us. Frankly, I don't know much about changing tires."

"Mr. Westmoreland, anyone who knows as much about law and helps people as much as you do, doesn't need to know how to change a tire. Step aside, young lady."

♫ ♫ ♫

The problem solved and back in the car, Ed sighed heavily. He shook his head in disbelief and turned to Beth.

"I think you could have changed the tire," he said and patted her shoulder.

She grinned. "Shows how brilliant you are, Mister Attorney. I was bluffing. I think we could've done it together. Might have taken us half the night, but we would have managed. I'll confess though, I was praying for help the whole time."

He laughed.

"Ed, I have another confession."

"Oh, oh." He shook his head. "What now?"

"I respect you. You admitted you didn't know how to change a tire. Most of the men I know would have been too macho to let that be known." Her voice quivered with admiration. "You are stuffy and as peculiar as my old maid Aunt Tillie, so I thought you'd be all puffy and try to cover up." She giggled. "Oh, I've said something stupid again!"

"Beth, my dear," he responded in a deep, oratorical voice, "I might be a pompous jerk, as you have been known to suggest, but I am scrupulously honest. Not humble, just honest."

When they arrived at her house, they were snickering like grade-school children.

Ben opened the door, looking at his watch, and grumbled, "I was getting worried."

He stared from one to the other, noting Ed's disheveled appearance.

"That lecture must have been a howling success."

"Brother of mine," Beth said, giggling again as she linked her arm under her companion's, "meet Honest Abe. He's not humble, but he is honest."

Ed bit his lip, looked down at his shoes, then lifted his chin and smiled sheepishly at Ben.

♫

♫

Chapter Thirteen

Joanna watched with concern as the driver attempted to park in front of her shop. He jumped the curb, and she glanced at her plate-glass window, but he reversed his action, shot back into the street, then jarred the car parked behind. He pulled forward again, jostling the car in front, and bounced back into place.

The bantam-sized man who climbed out of the old station wagon was not much taller than Beth. The sleeves of his blue-and-gray-plaid sports coat hung over his knuckles and dwarfed his shoulders. His bushy black mustache looked like a garish makeup prop glued to his upper lip.

From the back seat he pulled an oversized briefcase, then a large portfolio that he clutched against his chest. His stride to the shop was purposeful with quick, short steps. He set the briefcase down cautiously, as though it held solutions to the world's problems, and pushed open the door, which he held with his foot as he retrieved the briefcase.

Joanna stepped from her vantage point behind the counter. "Are you Percival Lineberger?"

"Yep. Call me Grip."

He stared at her through thick lenses, and from the expression on his face she guessed that her image appeared as distorted to him as his pale blue eyes were to her. The glasses magnified those eyes and exaggerated the length of his eyelashes.

Grip turned a slow complete circle, giving the shop a hasty perusal.

"Quaint," he said, "but it isn't . . ."

"Barnes and Noble."

"Treasures are seldom found in the big conglomerates." He eased his briefcase to the floor and extended his hand. It was then she understood how he earned the nickname "Grip."

"Welcome to The Gilded Teapot," she said. "This is Mrs. Burns, my new assistant. Come on back, and I'll show you the books. Ben plans to meet us at my father's office to evaluate the manuscript."

Grip nodded gravely to Mrs. Burns and bumped into the counter as he gathered his possessions to follow Joanna. She wondered how he had driven safely from Winston-Salem.

She had placed the books on a table in the back room. He extracted a large magnifying glass from his briefcase, then picked up each volume, checking for publication dates and noting the ones he could find. He studied the binding.

With each inspection he produced a strange rumbling sound from deep in his throat. "Um . . . ah . . . mummm . . ." Soon, he smiled. "Someone has taken excellent care of these."

When he had examined each book, he placed it in a neat pile, stacked according to size except for two volumes that he laid aside. "These," he informed Joanna, "are museum quality."

He studied a typed list he had taken from his portfolio, and a frown appeared unexpectedly.

"There's a book missing."

"There can't be." Joanna ran her hand around the interior of the box. "I unpacked them early this morning while Beth was still here to see them, because she was so interested."

"There are nine books on Ben's list, eight on the table. A possible autographed first edition of Andrew Lang's English translation of Homer's *The Iliad* – it's not here."

"Perhaps Ben moved it to his box. I'll check."

Joanna went into the closet and returned empty-handed. "I thought it was here earlier, but maybe we just miscounted." She told herself that she had no reason to be alarmed.

"Ben must have seen it if he listed it."

She smiled. "We'll have to ask him about it."

Grip Lineberger nodded thoughtfully. He pulled out a notebook and pursed his lips.

"I have a certified check made out for the total of nine books, using the prices I quoted Ben. Still, I can take these books back to my shop and sell them on consignment for possible higher bids."

He pointed to those he had designated as museum quality. "These two could go for a considerable amount."

He squinted at her. "Since there are only eight books, you might prefer that, although I can send you a corrected check tomorrow."

Joanna was perplexed. "Are you sure the other book is on Ben's list?"

"Yep. See? This is a printout of his list. I distinctly remember my interest in that particular edition. It would be a small volume, about four-and-a-half by six-and-a-half inches and about a half-inch thick."

She looked through the books again, then checked the closet and storage room once more. "Why don't you take them back and sell them for whatever you can?" she suggested. "I just want them out of here if they're that valuable."

She carefully locked the closet door, for the first time, before leaving the shop to go to the law offices with Grip.

Ben will have to come take the books he wants. I don't want to be responsible for them.

"Grip," she asked, "how much would you guess that copy of *The Iliad* could be worth?"

He paused and closed his eyes. "If it's a first edition in mint condition, and signed by Land himself, I'd guess somewhere in the thousands, possibly in the ten-thousands."

Those words had a chilling effect on Joanna.

♫

♫

Chapter Fourteen

A hush settled over the conference room at the law offices of Jerome and Westmoreland. Joanna, Ben, and Nicholas watched as the strange little man began his antics.

He took off his coat and draped it carefully over the back of a chair, then spread a large towel across the polished mahogany table. He ignored his audience as he unpacked paraphernalia from his brief-case – bottles of powder, some magnifying glasses, and tweezers in various sizes.

He nodded solemnly to Nicholas, who asked his secretary to bring the manuscript from the safe. Grip indicated a place on the table where he wanted the package. Before thanking the secretary, he asked her to remove the bouquet of flowers.

"Pollen and sprays could affect the paper."

The package lay unopened as the appraiser placed the tips of his fingers on the table and leaned toward the group. "Paper is made of layers of tiny interlocking fibers. The process was discovered by the Chinese," he began as though it was Papermak-ing 101.

He squinted at Joanna. "I've studied the photocopy you sent, and I have a few questions."

With spitfire rapidity, he hurled questions at them. He wanted to know where Mr. Henry obtained the manuscript, how long it had been in the shop, and if he was a member of the Porter family.

Joanna couldn't answer a single question. Nicholas knew only that his friend had moved to Galax Falls from Greensboro, where William Sydney Porter grew up.

Grip turned to Ben. "You're the literary expert. How did Porter spell his name?"

Ben gulped. "Come to think of it, I've seen Sydney spelled with an *i*. Is that important?"

"Sure is. It could tell us if this was written before or after he changed the spelling of his name. It could help pinpoint the date." Grip pulled on a pair of white cotton gloves, but did not touch the manuscript. He continued his interrogation of Ben. "How does this story compare to other O. Henry stories?"

"The style, subject matter dealing with ordinary people, and the surprise ending are all elements of O. Henry's stories."

Joanna was becoming impatient. She wanted Grip to get to the package.

As he fumbled with the newsprint that was wrapped around the manuscript, he said, "Give me the dates again."

Ben recited clipped answers. "Born eighteen sixty-two. Left Greensboro for Texas around eighteen ninety. Died in New York City in nineteen-ten. Enjoyed successful publications from around nineteen hundred."

"The best paper is made with rags. A German, Friedrich Keller, developed a way to make paper out of wood, and it has been successfully used in the United States since eighteen sixty-seven, so if we can prove that this is rag paper, it will tell us – what, Ben?"

Ben chuckled. "That is was written before eighteen sixty-seven."

Grip frowned. "Not necessarily. Rag paper is still in use. It *could* have been written before that date. But if it proves to be wood-based paper, it would eliminate the possibility that it was written before eighteen sixty-seven."

"Give Ben the dunce's hat," Nicholas teased and everyone – except Grip – laughed.

The little man seemed to forget anyone else was in the room. His attention was on the manuscript. He opened the folder and eased out the yellowed manuscript, touching it as little as possible.

Joanna barely breathed as she watched. Several minutes passed before she realized she was squeezing Ben's hand.

They watched, fascinated, as Grip performed all kinds of tests. Some he explained. With others, he worked too intently to be distracted by conversation. "We have developed a way to extract acids from old books and manuscripts to preserve them. Of course, I can't do that now." His movements were deliberate, precise. Gradually his posture changed. His shoulders seemed less rigid, his face more relaxed, and he became excited, pleased. He kept making the same strange sound he made in her shop, from deep in his throat. "Um . . . ah . . . mmm . . . "

He retrieved copies of cursive handwriting specimens from his portfolio, then picked up a magnifying glass and compared the manuscript to the sample. "If a writer habitually misspells a word, or uses unusual punctuation, or uses several favorite words and unique sentence patterns, those can be identifying tags. I'm not that much of an expert on Porter." He directed his attention to Ben again. "Are you?"

"No, sir. I have studied his work and life but I'm hardly an expert."

"We'll have to find an O. Henry expert. Now . . . let me tell you."

Joanna caught her breath.

"I can't prove this is a forgery. I can't prove it's genuine. I'm nearly sure it was written around the turn of the century or before, judging from the paper and the ink, but that doesn't mean that Porter actually wrote it. It's fancy handwriting for a man – too pretty."

"He was an artist," Ben said. "Did cartoons, illustrations."

"Yep. That could explain his handwriting. Several other possibilities exist. A family member might have copied one of his stories. Some hack could have copied his style and forged his name. It could be, though I doubt it, an out-and-out fake." He straightened his back and looked at each member of his audience as his words sank in.

Nicholas asked, "What do you think we should do with it?"

"I'd like permission to take it to New York and get an antique-manuscript professional and a literary specialist to evaluate it."

Nicholas nodded.

"Sir, I'm bonded," the little man said. "You can trust me."

"I don't doubt it for a minute," Nicholas assured him.

Grip reached back into his briefcase and withdrew a flat cardboard folder, which he deftly pushed into a box shape. "This is acid-free."

They watched as he placed the manuscript in the box and repacked his gear. He took off his white gloves, brushed his hands together and stared at Joanna. "Now. What about the missing book?"

"What missing book?" Nicholas asked.

Grip indicated Joanna with a nod of his head.

"Well . . . the list Ben sent to Grip included a book that we can't find," she explained. "I thought it was there earlier this morning, but when he examined the books, it wasn't there."

"Which book?" Ben asked, leaning forward in his chair.

"Andrew Lang's translation of – "

"*The Iliad*? I know that was there, because I recognized it as one of the more valuable volumes. I couldn't touch it, price wise, with a ten-foot pole. I think you had a copy in your shop once, Grip. You showed it to Beth and me."

"Yep. But it wasn't a first edition, or autographed. This one would be worth several thousand dollars if it's in good shape."

"Jo, honey," Nicholas asked, "what do you know about that woman you hired to help you in the shop?"

"Mrs. Burns? Not much. Actually, Beth recommended her. She worked for Mr. Henry and apparently knows a lot about antiques. She's your landlady, isn't she, Ben?"

"That's right."

"Let's not jump to any conclusions," Nicholas warned. "Perhaps the missing book will turn up."

Ben told Joanna, "I'll go back to the shop with you and help you look again."

♫

♫

Chapter Fifteen

"Thanks, Mrs. Burns. I'll close up."

Viola Burns, gray haired and matronly in her cotton and polyester smock, met them at the door. "I hope the gentleman from Winston-Salem was able to help you." She exuded a grandmotherly reassurance, though as the mother of a high schooler she was likely only in her late forties. Having her in the shop was a big help to Joanna.

Mrs. Burns went to the back of the store to get her purse and sweater. "I've had a rather busy afternoon, Joanna. I sold another teapot and also one of those pretty new cups."

She pulled her blue sweater around her shoulders and, dangling the huge purse on her arm, hurried to the back door. She stopped to chat with Ben. "I'll bet that little sister has surprised you, Mr. Benenson. She beats all I've ever seen."

"Yes, Ma'am," he said, "she takes the cake."

"And bakes it too!"

Mrs. Burns left laughing.

Ben searched the storage room and closet. "Did you look under the counter where the books were stored?" he said, his mouth tight with worry.

"No – but that space is full of a new shipment of cups and other china."

"Let's check."

She followed him to the front. "I'm not sure it matters so much, Ben. Dad thinks it will turn up. Grip said it is a small book. It would probably fit easily in a notebook or a purse."

"Or a diaper bag."

"What are you saying?"

The expression on Ben's face gave Joanna an uneasy feeling. He sighed. "I'm spouting off; ignore me." He took her hand and led her to the tables. "Beth was in trouble once before. Shoplifting. I don't want to believe she would be involved in this." He slumped down into a chair, looking as if he had aged ten years since he first entered the shop.

"I don't believe Beth took the book," Joanna said firmly.

"Of course not. She wouldn't do that – but, Joanna, kinda watch. If you ever find anything else missing, especially cash, will you let me know?"

She wanted to slip her arms around his neck and reassure him, but she felt irritated, too. They had so little time together. There was so much he kept promising to share with her, and the longing was tearing her apart. She didn't trust herself to answer without whining, so she only nodded.

"You didn't tell me what you thought of Grip." He was already heading toward the back door.

She took a step after him. "He's unusual . . . I expect he knows his business and there's so much money involved."

He turned around. "By the way, Joanna Jerome, let's take a hike on Saturday. Mister Ed – "

"Be nice."

"All right. Ed is taking Beth and Benjie to Grandfather Mountain. Something to do with otters and bears."

"Great! They're spending lots of time together." *More time together than we are,* she thought bitterly.

"She's crazy about him."

"How do you feel about it?"

"He's too much of a stuffed shirt for my taste. Seems almost magisterial – but if she likes him, it's okay with me, provided he doesn't break her heart." He laughed. "Did you hear about the flat tire?"

She shook her head, smiling, enjoying the sound of his laughter, anticipating the time he would spend telling it as much as the story.

"I'll tell you sometime. I promise."

"Empty promises – again," she retorted, too sharply.

He tilted his head and studied her, frowning.

"I guess you do get the short end of the stick – for now. Our dates won't always be confined to long walks and high-school football games. I'll call you tonight."

"Wait a minute!" She followed him to the door. He drew her into his arms and kissed her forehead. She leaned against him and whispered, "That's not what I had in mind."

"It's not what I want, either – I want much, much more! But – "

"Oh, Ben!" she exclaimed and pushed his arms away from her.

He gaped at her. "What on earth! You, of all people, should understand my situation. I have explained it to you – don't pressure me, please."

She blew up. "Pressure. *Pressure!* If that's what it is, just don't bother to come around."

Surprise could not begin to describe the reaction she saw in him. His mouth contorted; the color washed from his face. "Don't you *know* how I feel about you?"

"You've never told me." She was ashamed of the fretfulness in her voice, but she waited.

He wrapped her in his arms as though he could never let go. "I love you with all my heart. I just want to give you – so much more."

"I'll wait," she said meekly.

He kissed her then, and the passion in his kiss told her what he could never have explained to her in words.

♫ ♫ ♫

That evening Joanna had a long talk with her dad. She told him about Ben's suspicion that Beth could be involved with the missing book.

"Nonsense," he said flatly.

She explained about the shoplifting charge.

"Jo, I understand people. I've spent my life studying them. I'll bank on Beth. Now, what's really eating you?"

She shook her head. "Ben and I live in the same town, yet most of our conversation takes place over the phone, late at night. Dad, I must be very selfish."

"Because you want more time with Ben? Trust me, honey, you haven't a selfish bone in your body. You're in love, that's all, and it hasn't been a fair courtship. Not many young men take on the heavy obligations that Ben has. Seems to me that both of you are hampered by family liabilities."

She slipped her arms around his neck. "You are not my liability, Dad. You're firmly on the credit side of the account."

"You and Ben are going to make it just fine – but, honey, we never have enough time with our beloved." There was a catch in his voice. "Still, I'm pleased about Ben."

"He has never talked to me about marriage."

"Does he have to tell you? Everything about him yells out his love for you. He just has more than he can deal with right now."

"I wish Mother were here. She'd understand."

Softly he said, "I wish she were here, too. But, honey, I do understand. I'm just trying to say all the things a wise old sage should say. Keep your faith, kiddo."

♫

Chapter Sixteen

The parking lot at the beginning of the Rough Ridge Trail, just south of milepost 300 on the Blue Ridge Parkway, faced the waterfalls. The trail climbed up the mountain on the right of the falls, wound around to the left and crossed the top of the waterfalls on a small bridge. Joanna and Ben stood on the bridge and he looked across the vista beyond the Parkway.

Ben exclaimed, "Incredible!"

Joanna laughed. "Ah, you haven't seen anything yet."

Ben looked relaxed and handsome in his jeans and green-and-gray-plaid shirt with sleeves rolled up an inch or two. He carried a knapsack across his shoulders. "Do you know all these trails along the Parkway?"

"Most of them. Dad was a great hiker. Our family used to backpack together – Mom, Dad, Andy, and me." She saw the longing in his eyes and wondered about his childhood.

They followed the trail to where it turned to wind through a hemlock and maple grove and sloped upward. "Here's my favorite spot for jack-in-the-pulpits down under the conifers. They've died back for fall, but those shiny, dark green round leaves are galax. They turn a gorgeous bronze color in the winter and make wonderful wreaths. The tall blue flowers are gentian. And, see the slender stalks with five round leaves? That's ginseng, called *sang* by the natives who've lived here all their lives – "

Ben interrupted. "You mean the herb used in Chinese folk medicine?"

She nodded. "Just a few years ago it was selling for three hundred dollars a pound!"

"I'm interested in that plant. I've heard it has aphrodisiac powers. Perhaps I'd better dig some up. Might help my love life."

She laughed. "Don't think so! It would likely land you in jail. It's been so over-harvested that it's now a protected species. You don't want to be caught poaching plants, especially ginseng on the Parkway."

"What are those really pretty red leaves over by the tree trunk?"

"Don't touch that – it's poison oak. It *is* pretty."

He took her arm, and laughing, marched on.

"I can't imagine growing up in a place like this," he said with wonder as they walked side by side, "or taking hikes with my father."

Joanna had been pleased by his exuberance. Now she was distressed by the suggestion of his barren childhood. Hers had been happy.

The broad trail left the wooded area as it snaked upward. "The park service has done a great job of engineering, don't you think?" she asked.

He nodded, then shook his head in disbelief. "It's fantastic."

"Tell me about your growing up."

Ben didn't show any sign of running out of breath on the climb, so far. She wondered how they would fare on the rougher part of the hike.

"Not much to tell," he said. "There were five of us, all nearly grown when Beth came along – as a tremendous surprise. We didn't have much of a family life. We were encouraged to get out and find jobs as early as possible. I was lucky to find a good church group and a choir. I left home as soon as I could; we all did. Most married unsuccessfully, like Beth. I spent several summers working out west on ranches until I left for college, but I was always especially close to Beth. I might not have come back at all except for her."

"Didn't your parents want her?"

"I don't think that was it. They just hadn't expected another child. My mother was forty-two when Beth was born, and Dad was already failing. He had his first stroke at forty-five – and Beth wasn't the easiest kid to raise."

"I suspect she sensed she was not welcome," Joanna said sadly.

Smooth plank steps, with protective handrails along the ledges, required little effort on the leisurely hike, and Joanna was able to watch Ben's enjoyment of the scenery. She realized that he was expecting a more strenuous hike, and she waited for his reaction.

She pointed out the species of various trees and wild flowers. "The turkey beard is spectacular here in the early summer."

"Turkey beard?"

"It's a tall white clustered flower that grows from a grasslike clump. They're pretty rare, but there are more on this path than any other place I know. The deer love to chew on them."

"What's this little stubby-looking plant?"

"Sand myrtle. They stay small up here. You've likely seen them growing much taller on the beach."

They had reached a broad platform with benches to give hikers a rest with an incomparable view of the mountain range. "I never saw anything this elaborate on a trail," Ben said. He turned to look back over the endless blue horizon and took a deep breath. "Oh, Joanna . . . may it never become ordinary to me! Just smell this clean air! I don't know if my old city lungs can take it."

She laughed. "Now we start our hike."

He joined her in laughter. "I was wondering what kind of hike this was."

"Look up there. See that outcropping of rocks? Let's go up. We are only part of the way."

They had walked side by side, but the trail – if it could still be called a trail – was different here. It required moving single-file, twisting and winding upward among cliffs and rocks. Trees showed worn spots, the bark damaged and rubbed away by many hands. Rocks were marked and chipped from hikers' boots. Ben led the way, reaching back to help Joanna over the roughest spots.

The view was breathtaking – waves of mountains melding into distant sky. The beat of broad wings – an eagle perhaps – sounded from somewhere nearby. Joanna's attention followed that sound; she slipped and caught at a rock to keep from falling. Ben turned, bracing against a tree trunk and grabbed at her arm, white faced.

"I must be insane for allowing you to come up here," Ben said. "What if you fell? And look – you've hurt your hand? I'm not sure a musician should even be allowed on this trail."

Joanna laughed. "*I* brought *you* – remember?" She sucked at the spot of blood on her finger. "But you're right, I should have brought gloves. I forgot – distracted by the prospect of your company, I guess."

"Do you want to go back? We can come another day with the right equipment." He craned his neck to look up the trail. "Ropes and slings it looks like from here."

"Not a chance. We're almost there."

In some areas the path had been carved deeply by thousands of hikers, but often it was merely marked with yellow paint on rough rocks they had to scale. They were breathless when they came to the final clearing.

"Look at this massive rock!" Ben exclaimed. "Does the path end here?"

"No, see, that other fork goes cross-country, but I don't think I can go much further today."

"Okay. What about a backpack trip up here sometime? With tents and food." He turned around and looked out across the dozens of ridges, the mist in the valleys creating the illusion of choppy ocean waves. "Oh, honey! Look, you can see Linn Cove Viaduct! The curves are so graceful from up here. And right above it, isn't that about where the swinging bridge is on Grandfather Mounain?" he said.

He raised his eyes back up to the mountain over the ridge, his gaze sliding up to the peak. "I guess Ed and Beth and Benjie are up there on Grandfather by now. I wonder what's happening between those two. They spend every Saturday together. They drove to Hickory last week to buy a special kind of car seat so they won't have to keep taking the one out of my car."

"Dad gets tickled every time he sees that car seat in Ed's BMW." Joanna glanced up and thought about the unlikely trio. Only her dad had foreseen that miracle. She wished he could have come with them today. "Dad used to tell me that this trail represents life. It's full of hidden views and twists and turns and uncertainty. You never know what might be ahead, and it's a hard climb. There are mountaintops and valleys just like the ups and downs in life."

After she said it, she was a bit embarrassed by the philosophical speech that tumbled from her, but he seemed to appreciate it.

"I can hardly wait to bring Benjie up here when he's older," he said.

Joanna sat down on flat gray granite rock, and he sat beside her.

"Yesterday after school, and after the rain, I took him out on the deck. Do you know what that little rascal said to me? 'Catch me rainbow, Uncle Ben. Catch me rainbow.' Can you believe it?"

"We saw a spectacular rainbow up here once.

It arced over the Parkway to the east. It was the day after Mother's diagnosis of cancer, and we thought it was a good omen." There was a catch in her voice. For a moment she sat very still, then asked, "Did you explain to Benjie about rain dust?"

"Benjie doesn't need a walk in the rain to get his life in perspective." He grinned at her and spread his arms wide, pivoting from the waist and sweeping the whole scene below him. "This is as spectacular an experience as catching a rainbow. Thanks."

"I didn't give it to you. As I recall, you climbed up yourself. There's just a hint of color change now, but wait till you see it in the full fall colors – and in the snow."

"I look forward to hikes in every season with you, Joanna," he said quietly, almost reverently. "You are particularly lovely with a view of the Blue Ridge Mountains behind you."

He reached behind him for his knapsack. "This is the most elegant dining room I've ever been in. Have a pickle."

"I'm glad you thought to bring a lunch. It was sweet of Beth to fix the sandwiches."

"We were wrong about Ed, incidentally," Ben said. "They've found a favorite McDonald's in Elizabethton – one with an indoor playground." He chuckled. "Beth tells me he's careful to insist that Benjie washes his hands carefully before he eats – especially if he's been playing in the area with all the balls."

They laughed, enjoyed their simple meal and studied the vista together.

"I used to dream about being a mountain climber," Joanna said. "I read every book in the library about mountain climbing and rock climbing.

Do you know what a handhold called a 'Thank Godder' is?"

He shook his head, watching her intently.

"On difficult trips rock climbers search for foot and handholds to traverse the faces of dangerous rocks. On the steepest, most hazardous ones, a handhold that has enough space for the climber to sink his fingers in and get grip and lifesaving support is called a 'Thank Godder.'"

"I like that." He took another deep breath. "It's beautiful up here. Awesome. And I like the guide's dialogue. I love every minute I spend with you."

She dropped her gaze to the little red wintergreen plants around the rocks. She had bad news for Ben some time on this trip, but she dreaded telling it to him. She didn't want anything to mar the magical spell of intimacy that drew them together.

They had enjoyed having the trail to themselves, but now they heard other hikers on their way up. Joanna told herself that the trip down could be dangerous if Ben were upset or preoccupied about Beth. Even though waiting was a delaying tactic, she yielded to it.

It was far more difficult going down than coming up. Joanna sat on the rocks and slid down several rough passages, much to the delight of a couple of youngsters on the trail with their parents. When they reached the wooden platform, they stopped to rest.

"Are you worn out, honey?" Ben asked. "You're terribly quiet. I think it's more than fatigue."

She gave him a brave smile, and he drew her arm under his as they started down the wider trail. He persisted. "What's wrong?"

"Lorlene Burns has been working in the shop

all week, helping her mother after school. What do you know about her at the high school?"

"Not much. She seems popular – particularly with the boys. She's a fair student, not academically ambitious. Is she a problem?"

Joanna took a deep breath. "Well – *someone's* a problem."

"Oh?"

"You asked me to keep you posted. Several small items are missing from the store, and cash, too."

The change in him was sudden. His shoulders drooped, his eyes looked wretched and tired. His voice dropped to such a low pitch that she had to strain to hear his brusque question. "How much cash?"

She wondered if he was blaming her. He seemed annoyed.

"Only twenty dollars. Ten dollars at a time."

"Does it happen when Beth is there?" he asked angrily.

"Ben, I can't tell."

"But *after* my sister has been there?" His stance, even the way he dropped his hands to his sides, was full of resignation.

"You know she delivers the rolls, has tea with me, and often serves a couple of people just for fun."

"What else is missing?"

"Nothing terribly expensive, except the book. Some nice pieces of silverware and at least one antique saucer. The little tin antique toy, Kermit the frog – it's gone. It's probably not worth much, but it means a lot to me. Dad and Benjie make a huge game out of it."

"Yes. Beth told me."

He stopped on the trail, looking so forlorn that she wanted to throw her arms around him and say it didn't matter, that Beth could have everything in the store – but she knew it did matter. It was the matter of trust.

Finally he asked, "Are all the missing things from the antique collection?"

"Well . . . yes. I hadn't thought about that, but I bought them all from Mr. Henry."

"Are the books still locked safely in the closet?"

"Of course, Ben."

"I don't know if I should confront Beth yet."

Joanna stepped in front of him and forced him to face her. "We don't know anything yet. I wish I had never mentioned it, but you asked me to. Come home with me and talk to Dad."

He moved around her and hurried on ahead. He waited for her at the car and silently held the door for her. Joanna could hardly believe this was the same joyful, joking man who started the hike with her less than two hours earlier. And in a way, it was her fault.

"Come talk with Dad," she insisted.

"Not yet. I have to work this out. God help us if she messes up her life again. I saw the vitality sucked out of her once – but I can't stand back and let her wreck Benjie's life, or mine. Our parents always believed that she was involved in her husband's crime rampage."

"Ben, Listen to me – Mrs. Burns and Lorlene have been around the shop, and Mrs. Burns claims to understand the value of antiques. So far Beth isn't implicated at all."

"But Mrs. Burns and Lorlene don't have a record for stealing."

"Ben – "

"I'm fed up. Disgusted. Sick! I have failed her

again, it seems. I've got to get home to weed out this whole sordid mess. I'll search the house before Beth comes home."

When they reached her home, he wouldn't go in. "I'd be embarrassed to see your father."

"Will I see you tomorrow?" Joanna asked.

"At this point I can't promise anything. I'm sorry."

"Surely," she said to his retreating back, "you don't blame yourself! You behave almost as though you hold *me* responsible, like you're looking for someone – anyone – to blame."

He was gone.

♫

♫

Chapter Seventeen

"Come on, Ed!" Beth wiggled her fingers, stretched between the exuberant Benjie and beckoning to Ed, who seemed rooted beside the door of the BMW.

"I'll wait for you in the Visitor Center," Ed said, motioning toward the three-story block-like building across the parking lot below the summit of Grandfather Mountain.

"There's no point in coming all the way to the top and stopping in the parking lot. I mean, just because you can't get there in your fancy car – "

"What about Benjie – ?"

"I'm holding his hand. He's fine."

In the end Ed yielded – reluctantly – following them up the stone steps the last dozen yards to the top of Grandfather Mountain. He stopped at the bronze plaque set in the step at exactly one mile of altitude, brushing the stone wall on the left with his knuckles.

Now, standing on the huge boulder that supported the bridge, Beth couldn't imagine having missed it. A thin wisp of a limpid cloud hung below them, and beneath the undulating mist, shades of green and gold, boxes of buildings and cars, the winding silver ribbon of the highway, and in the distance ripples upon ripples of lesser mountains extended as far as she could see. A tremor of excitement crawled up the backs of her legs. This was as close to flying as she had ever been.

She gazed down on a soaring raven, its powerful black wings hang-gliding in the air currents off Grandfather Mountain. A hawk floated across the mountain, as exotic a sound to her as a screaming macaw in the Amazon. When she turned to gaze behind her, the higher gray peaks of the mountain poked through the white clouds. She caught her breath as the wind slapped the collar of her red windbreaker against her cheeks.

"Ed, why on earth did you try to avoid bringing me up here? I love it!"

She read a sign out loud:

"BE CAREFUL ON THIS RUGGED MOUNTAIN.
AVOID LEDGES, STORMS, AND HIGH WINDS.
WATCH FOOTING.
SUPERVISE CHILDREN."

Ed stared at the ground as if he were angry with her. "Benjie, hold tight to your mother's hand."

The unusual quaver in Ed's voice brought her attention completely upon him. He looked ashen as he pulled his hat tighter down on his head. His outfit – a yellow shirt and tan slacks with vest and brown suede jacket – was not designed for a mountain hike. He clutched the lapels of his jacket as though he were freezing to death.

"Ready to go?" he asked.

"Go? We just got here!"

"I need to. I brought you to see the animals."

Benjie tugged on her windbreaker. "Mommy. Sing. Bridge sing."

She paused and listened. "Yes, it does! Ed, do you hear that? The whistle? Benjie says the bridge is singing."

He didn't seem to hear her.

"Well, I won't leave without crossing that swinging bridge. Aren't you coming?"

"No. Anyway, it's not supposed to swing much since the recent renovation."

"So, what's stopping you? I'm going!" She quivered with anticipation as she hurried to the tower of the bridge. She read the posted sign aloud:

ELEVATION FIVE THOUSAND, THREE HUNDRED FIVE FEET.
ONE MILE HIGH.
LIMIT: FORTY PERSONS

Taking Benjie's hand in hers, she turned back to say, "Don't be a killjoy, Ed. Come across with us. I thought we were going to do something nice together. Are you a coward?"

"Yes."

"But look at the cables. They must be nearly two inches in diameter."

Ed just shook his head, tight-lipped.

Trying to suppress her impatience and disappointment, Beth stepped on the bridge, holding tight to Benjie's hand. It moved just a bit, and an exhilarating tingle spread through her, raising goose pimples up her spine. Below, the variegated green shades of balsam fir, spruce, mountain laurel, and rhododendron swayed as something moved through them in a line. *Could it be one of the famous Grandfather Mountain bears?* They had already spotted three deer, and a fat gray grouse flew over the roof of the car on the way up, much to Benjie's delight. But surely the bears were all in the habitat. She heard a slight creak as they slowly eased forward on the bridge, and she leaned over the thick cable handrail for a better look.

"Please don't do that . . ." Ed's voice sounded strange.

"Do what?" Beth checked Benjie but he was resting his chin on the railing, the fingers of his free hand wound around the cable. He seemed fine – as transfixed by the view as she was.

"Don't lean over the side like that."

Beth shrugged, and walked with exaggerated care toward the middle of the bridge, until they stood suspended above a deep crevice in the rock. The sign read:

ONE MILE UP

Suspended in space, she was too excited to study the details. She twisted around to glance back at Ed and tell him, "It's only two hundred twenty-eight feet long. And look, there's a rock peak on the other side. I bet the view is unbelievable from there."

He watched, standing in the exact spot where she'd left him, and did not move to join them.

"Kitty!" Benjie shrieked with laughter, pointing, and Beth watched with him as a large raccoon appeared over the far end of the bridge, climbing hand over hand up the wire like an agile acrobat. It dropped to the floor and ambled off into the bushes.

"Ed!" Benjie called. "Come!"

Ed ignored him, deliberately looking toward the stairs to the parking lot.

"Ed. You didn't even look at the raccoon!"

"Don't be silly, Beth. Raccoons are nocturnal."

"I don't care what they are *not*. We saw one, with its cute black robber mask and everything."

"Well, stay away from it." Ed glanced up at them, then stared at his own feet. "If it's out in the daytime, there may be something wrong with it."

Suddenly Benjie broke away from her and raced back toward Ed. She grabbed at the side-rail and started after him, but tripped and fell to her knees.

Ed waved at him frantically, mutely begging him to go back, but Benjie surged on. The child staggered on the uneven path, stumbled, and fell at his feet. Ed scooped him up and examined him for injuries. He brushed him off and carefully set Benjie on his feet, heading him back toward the bridge. "Go with your mother."

Benjie spread his feet and said obstinately, "No. Ed come."

Beth saw consternation wash over Ed's face. "I'll take you back to the bridge," he said. Ed took one step onto the bridge and leaned into the wind like a long, lank figurehead on an old sailing ship. The breeze whipped his jacket.

"Go on, Benjie," he said impatiently. He held the boy's hand as far onto the bridge as he could reach.

"No. Benjie scared."

Ed slid his left foot forward, clinging to the railing. "Come get him, Beth."

Some prankish impulse took hold of her, and she scampered farther out onto the bridge. "Ed! Come on out."

A sudden gust of wind whisked Ed's hat into the air, lifting it and tossing it around. It tumbled and fell away into space like an escaped kite.

Beth saw him shudder. "Come on, Ed. The bridge will hold forty men like you."

His chalk-like face was pinched with anxiety as he navigated one or two timorous steps in an awkward dragging motion, sliding his feet onto the deck of the bridge without lifting them. Then he recoiled and grappled frantically with the handrails, shaking noticeably.

Beth watched, stunned into stillness, as Ed regained his equilibrium and made one more feeble effort to move onto the planks of the bridge. A clammy feeling gripped her throat, and for an instant in her mind's eye she saw Ed, off balance, toppling over and plunging into the rock ravine.

"Wait!" she screamed. "I'm coming back!"

"Don't rock the bridge!"

Keeping the bridge as steady as she could, she walked slowly toward them. At five feet, one inch tall, she was short enough that the railings gave her a sense of security, but they were scant protection to Ed, whose eyes were sunk deep in the sockets of his pale face. His knuckles were white as he clung to the railing. He had managed to go a couple of feet onto the bridge, and he panted, as if he were going to pass out.

Thoroughly alarmed, Beth scanned the area for assistance. They had met other visitors descending as they came up the steps, but they were alone on the mountain now. If she screamed, no one would hear her over the wind. She dared not leave Ed to get help.

It was up to her. She barely came to Ed's shoulder, and he outweighed her two to one. She sent up as frantic a prayer as she had ever prayed in her life, then put her arm around his waist and slipped up under his left arm. He was as rigid as the bridge tower and about as maneuverable.

He gripped the rail with his left hand, still clutching Benjie's hand with his right.

"Ed. Turn around. Let go of the rail and put your left hand on my shoulder."

"I can't."

"Yes, you can. Hold on to me."

He remained paralyzed.

"Listen to me, Ed. You must trust me. Let go of the rail and turn around. Benjie, you turn around, slowly."

Benjie didn't understand. She nudged him with her leg. "Help Mommy, Benjie. Let's help Ed off the bridge."

The child, responding to the tone of her voice, began an unsteady hundred eighty-degree turn, and Ed pivoted with him, allowing Beth to support and steer him. He released Benjie's hand and grabbed the rail with his right hand, then took a deep breath. They began the short trek toward the tower, inching painfully along the steel planks of the bridge. The two or three feet they had to cross seemed to stretch for miles. Benjie attempted to push him from behind with his little hands on Ed's hips.

Ed was shaking and gasping for breath when Beth helped him to the bench near the bridge tower. He was covered with sweat in spite of the cool wind. "I'm so ashamed," he whispered. "I was helpless."

Beth faced him with a hand on each of his shoulders. "Are you all right, Ed?" she asked, her voice trembling. She brushed the hair back from his forehead and gently framed his face with her hands. She clasped the frames of his glasses and pushed them back up on his ears from where they had slipped. He was watching her with a look of aching anguish.

"I'm sorry about your hat," she said, then leaned over impulsively and kissed his forehead.

"Ah," he sighed, "what strength in infirmity. I should have explained that I have acrophobia."

She sat down beside him. "Oh. I just thought you were afraid of heights."

He shook his head and managed a weak smile. "Beth, sweet one, that's what acrophobia is." He stayed hunched, leaning against her a moment until his breathing became regulated. "I'm so embarrassed. It was excruciating. It's difficult enough for me to climb up the steps, but I didn't want to disappoint you. You may have saved my life. That must have been awful for you."

"Ed scared?" Benjie climbed up on the bench, his dark eyes full of distress, his soprano voice quivering in concern as he studied him. "Benjie scared." He patted Ed's leg.

Ed worked his mouth self-consciously, apparently incapable of expressing his emotions. He looked shyly at the little boy and turned to Beth.

She stroked his shoulder, her heart filled with tenderness. "Ed, I guess you are human after all."

He raised his eyebrows quizzically.

"I was wrong to insist we come here," she said.

He struggled to articulate. Finally he put one arm around Benjie and the other around Beth. "Bless you both."

A moment later he said, "I guess you'll want me to take you on home now."

"Are you kidding? I know what fear is. At least you have a fancy name for yours. I'm just afraid of eyes in the dark, for one thing."

"Eyes?"

"I'm scared to death that I'll see eyes peering at me from the darkness in the closet, at the window, or under the bed. You ask Ben. He'll tell you I sometimes make him come into my room and look under the bed before I can go to sleep. Let's go see the bears now."

"Benjie see bear."

♬ ♬ ♬

There was no further mention of Ed's ordeal as they toured the animal habitat. He bought a small sack of dried apples for Benjie to throw to the bears, and when the crowd of people made it too hard for the boy to see the cubs, Ed hoisted him to his shoulders. Fortunately, Ed was tall enough that he could stand back from the low rock wall between the tourists and the cliff surrounding the bear habitat.

Benjie kept hold of Ed's hand as they watched the otters. The child laughed delightedly at the antics of the agile animals.

"See the eagles?" Ed said. "They can't fly, so they live here where they can be safe."

"Eagles scared?"

Ed knelt beside him. "Afraid to fly? No. They are not like Ed, afraid of heights. They've been hurt."

Beth, watching the two together, was filled with a sudden curious yearning. She tried to brush it aside. She would not make a fool of herself just because Ed was kind to her son.

"Let's eat lunch here," Ed suggested as they headed back toward the museum. "The outside tables aren't crowded now."

They had the deck to themselves.

"I heard a couple talking about what a cute family we are," Beth said, giggling, as she cut Benjie's sandwich.

"I heard it too," Ed replied. "Did that embarrass you?"

"I loved it. How about you?"

"I loved it." He gave her a shy glance before looking again at his plate. "I'll have to get a red windbreaker like yours so we'll match." He chuckled at the thought.

Beth smiled. "Ed, why haven't you ever gotten married?"

He gagged on his coffee and dribbled liquid across his sleeve. "That's a shocking question out of the clear blue sky."

"I've been wondering about it for some time."

"Actually, I haven't asked anyone in several weeks."

She giggled again and turned to study him. "You're such a wonderful man. You'd be such a good husband and father – for somebody."

He looked at his plate and glanced at her out of the corner of his eye. "Would you marry me?"

"Me?"

She laughed, but he didn't. She stopped abruptly with a catch in her throat. "You *are* kidding?"

"Must be a good joke. You're sure laughing about it. I'm not usually that humorous."

She clapped her hands over her mouth, and her eyes widened. "You're *not* kidding?" She was astounded. "But I'm just a brat, following you around like a kid sister."

"Would the idea be that distasteful?"

"Oh, Ed, you are the most wonderful man I've ever been around." She picked up her Coke cup, then put it back down. She couldn't seem to catch her breath. "You *are* kidding, aren't you?"

Ed shook out his napkin and brushed coffee off his sleeve. "No. I'm not much of a kidder. I hadn't meant to ask you so bluntly. Perhaps we haven't been dating long enough to think about marriage."

Dating? She had enjoyed their friendly relationship but had not regarded it as dating, except the night he took her to Boone for dinner and to hear the lecture about owls. They had watched a few old Jimmy Stewart movies together at her house. He sat with her in church and took them for long Saturday afternoon rides, but she had not realized –

"Ed, I just thought you were being kind. I couldn't imagine your being interested in me romantically. I never considered myself your equal."

"Why not? Of course you're my equal."

"In many ways I'm just a street brat – with a kid to support and some other major problems."

"Just think about it. I won't rush you. I know I'm happier with you – with you and Benjie – than I've ever been in my life. I'm not very romantic. I seem to turn women off . . . but I love you, Beth, and together we could make a home for Benjie."

She was silent.

"Remember the evening you brought me dinner?" he asked.

"I took you leftovers from a catering party."

"You set the table for one in my apartment, and then you left. It was the loneliest night of my life."

"I wanted to do something nice for you," she said, "but I wasn't sure you like quiche, and I didn't want to embarrass you."

"I wanted you to stay and eat with me. I didn't want you to leave – ever."

"I didn't know! Oh, Ed." She took a deep breath and gazed at him thoughtfully. "You have so much to offer, and I'd only bring embarrassment to you."

"No, Beth. I'm the one who embarrasses you with my pomposity – let's call it what it is. I come across as haughty when I don't mean to. There are a lot of things about me that probably turn you off." He folded his napkin, then spread it out again.

"I've fantasized about you from that first day I saw you at Joanna's shop," she said, "when I teased you so unmercifully."

"I thought you were a total psychopath."

"So, why'd you offer to help me with the posters the next time you saw me?"

Ed grinned. "You were so pathetic, helpless."

Beth bit her lip. "That's funny. It wasn't until you became so pathetically helpless today that I realized how special you are to me. You never needed me before."

Ed arched his eyebrows, tilted his head, and gazed at her. "I always need you, Beth. In every way. You give me a whole new reason for existence. You keep my feet on the ground."

"Mommy, more catsup?" Benjie said. "Please?"

"Ed, you don't know what you're getting into. You don't know about my background."

"Mommy . . . ?" a small voice pleaded again.

"I've told you a little about the way I messed up my life, big time. I had a terrible marriage and a nasty divorce."

"I said please," Benjie persisted.

Ed tilted the bottle and poured a little round of red catsup onto Benjie's plate beside his fries. "How's that, Benjie?" To Beth, he said, "How can you say you've messed up your life when you produced Benjie?"

Her eyes filled with tears.

"Thanks, Ed." She tried to take a sip of her Coke, but her hand was shaking. "You're a high-class lawyer. I'm a girl with a past. I'm impulsive, impetuous. I dropped out of high school my senior year, and you have advanced college degrees."

"You give me what I don't have."

She laid down her sandwich, covered her mouth with her fingertips, and closed her eyes a moment. "Listen, Ed," she said quietly, "I don't know how to tell you – what if . . . what if I had a criminal record?"

"What if *I* did?"

"Don't be silly. Go read my rap sheet. Maybe

it's not complete. Suppose I'm in some trouble now that I can't explain." Her voice became husky. "Suppose I'm about to bring disgrace on Ben and everyone who knows me?" She looked at her plate, and a lock of blonde hair fell across her face.

"I can't imagine anything that could make a difference in the way I feel about you – and I *have* read your rap sheet. I looked it up when you asked me to get you a gun. It doesn't matter. That was a long time ago."

She jerked up her head and stared at him.

"You've read my rap sheet, and you still spend time taking Benjie and me places?" She swallowed. "You could be in court in a few weeks defending me for something I can't tell you about. Do you want a relationship with a potential criminal client?"

"Don't talk like that. We're working on the telephone threats and protection for Benjie." He covered her hand with his. "If there's something else, I wish you'd discuss it with me."

She shook her head.

Gently he brushed the strand of hair from her face and sighed. "Forget about this until we get everything straightened out – but I'll ask you again."

Beth tried to smile, but her lips quivered. Ed was looking at her with such intensity that she became self-conscious. She looked at her sandwich. "I'm going to hold you to that, dear Ed."

♫

♫

Chapter Eighteen

Joanna returned from the hike filled with alarm. *Is my life going to fall apart again?*

The thefts were causing consternation for everyone dear to her. She had watched her father's response with a growing concern, and it scared her. Ben's reaction surprised her.

It was her shop, her responsibility. She had to solve the problem herself. She decided to catch the thief. Praying for wisdom, she reviewed several options. She carefully brainstormed every idea she could think of, and she believed she had the answer.

She placed a phone call to Grip Lineberger.

♫ ♫ ♫

Sunday afternoon Joanna answered the door at the first tone of the bell. She had hoped Ben would come. He was distant and preoccupied after church, barely speaking to her. She looked at him through the glass. His shoulders were rigid, his eyes downcast. When she opened the door, he reached between the screen and door jamb to hand her something.

"I found it under the front seat of the car," he said and turned to leave.

Joanna looked down in her palm at the small toy. It was the little frog. Her heart dropped to her stomach. "Ben . . ." she whispered.

He raised his hand in a slight wave and continued toward his car. She followed him, letting the door slam behind her.

"Just a minute! Just a cotton-picking minute." She stalked after him, spitting out each syllable of her words. "You stop right there!"

Ben could not have looked more surprised if she had thrown ice water in his face. "What?"

"Now, you just listen to me. Don't you walk away without talking to me about this. I care too much for Beth – and you – for you to walk out on me this way." Her throat felt as if it was closing up; she could not remember when she had been so angry or frustrated. Furthermore, Joanna Jerome did not yield to the pressures of life. "If you won't talk with me, then at least speak with Dad. What's wrong with you anyway?"

When she yanked on his hand, he followed her like a docile little boy into the house. Nicholas, hearing the ruckus, had shuffled slowly toward the front door. As they came in, he moved out of their way to let them pass, then followed them through the hall into the den.

Joanna stood with her arms folded across her chest. "Ben, sit down."

He sank into a chair.

Nicholas chuckled. "Sorry, son. I can't do a thing with her when she gets like this."

He set aside his walker and sat in the armchair facing Ben. "From what I gather, she's holding you against your will. You have the right to counsel if you want it."

Ben took a deep breath, then shrugged. "I didn't think she'd want to see me ." He did not look at Joanna.

"That's insulting," she said and found a chair at the far end of the room. "I'm not that shallow."

"Okay!" Nicholas said. "Hush – both of you – and pay attention."

The silence was deafening. The den became a courtroom. "What proof do you have that Beth is dipping into the till?"

Joanna cleared her throat. Ben looked at his shoes. Nicholas whacked his palm against his walker, rattling it back against the wall. Joanna jumped, and Ben flinched.

"You know what's wrong?"

Joanna and Ben stared at Mr. District Attorney.

"You two are scared to death. Afraid that some little thing is going to come between you and split you up. Is your relationship that fragile?"

"Dad!"

Ben leaned forward to stand up. "Sir, with all due respect, I think – "

"Sit down. You think *what*?"

Ben gulped and slumped back into his chair.

"That's the whole problem. Neither of you is thinking *at all*." His eyes bored into them.

Ben gaped at him. Joanna swallowed, and it hurt her throat. She had not realized she was that tense. The two of them avoided eye contact with each other, their attention riveted on Nicholas.

"Jo, you have been, until recently, almost unflappable and logical in your conclusions. Ben, you strike me as superior in every way – intellectually, morally, spiritually. So how do you explain this drivel?" He glared at them, his eyes smoldering.

Joanna spoke first. "D-dad . . . cash and merchandise have been disappearing."

"Have you seen Beth take anything?"

"Of course not."

Nicholas turned to address Ben. "Have you found any evidence at your house to connect her to the thefts? I assume you searched."

Ben nodded.

"What? Only the little tin toy frog in the car," Nicholas recited in a singsong rhythm. "Little tin toy frog."

In prime courtroom form, he frowned at each of them. They were reduced to putty. "Who else has been in that car?"

Before either of them could speak, he leaned his weight on the walker and stood up. He counted on his left hand. "Benjie . . . you . . . Jo . . . " Nicholas waited while the message sank in.

He pointed one long thin finger at his daughter. "Did you or did you not mention that Beth drove Lorlene home one afternoon?"

"Yes, sir." She moistened her lips. "She did."

Ben spoke up. "I don't know what to say."

"Let's formulate a plan of action," Nicholas said. "Jo, you had an idea last night. Explain it."

"I just thought . . . that . . . maybe . . ."

"Speak up!"

Joanna hiccuped. Ben shifted in his seat but didn't make a sound.

Joanna giggled, then started sputtering. Her laughter became full blown, until tears flowed down her cheeks. "Dad, you scoundrel!"

She staggered to the couch, and when she sat down, Ben moved over to sit beside her. He put his arm around her, and together they faced her father, waiting expectantly for instructions.

Ben's whipped-dog look was gone. His eyes were bright with hope, and he wiggled his shoulders in anticipation. He had not questioned Nicholas's tactics.

"I may be a scoundrel," Nicholas said, beaming, "but my method worked. You two are huddled together, holding hands, and thinking about how to catch the real thief."

They smiled at each other self-consciously.

Joanna said, "I thought about setting a trap. I don't think Beth is a thief. I just want to find out who is."

"Good," Nicholas said. "Explain your plan to Ben."

Joanna remembered how much her father's clients had always loved him, and she knew why.

♬ ♬ ♬

Much later, as they sat at the table with bowls of hot soup, Ben confessed, "I've never known a man like you, Nicholas. You put me through the wringer this evening. You scared me to death – but you have given me a renewed faith."

He smiled at Joanna. "On our hike Joanna explained about the handholds that a rock climber needs. Sir, tonight you became my handhold, my 'Thank Godder.'"

"That's quite a compliment. Thank you. All you needed to do was to have a little faith in your sister."

"Nicholas, someday when all this is over, I hope to ask permission to become your son-in-law."

"If you have the courage, or little enough sense, to suggest that after watching my daughter in action earlier this evening, you'll get no dissension from me. I wouldn't dare cross her."

"She's a lot like you, Nicholas."

Joanna rolled her eyes. "I may just marry Edward Westmoreland."

Nicholas coughed lightly. "Honey, I have the distinct impression Ed is no longer available."

"Then I guess I'll just be an old maid."

Ben winked at Nicholas, and his lips twitched. "Pass the chili sauce."

♫

♫

Chapter Nineteen

Joanna's concert days were on an indefinite hiatus, but the poise and courage developed from years on the musical stage were about to be tested. She was confident at an organ or piano keyboard, because she knew what to do there. Today she was treading new waters; her goal was to trap a thief.

As she prepared, she was drawn into the intrigue of the adventure. There was more at stake than the monetary considerations. Her hands trembled as she buttoned her blouse and fumbled with her brush, dropping it twice.

The sun was just beginning to spread across the mountains, like the opening curtain at a theater, when she pulled out of the driveway. She was not accustomed to the early hour and had forgotten how beautiful the little town was before people began to stir. Smoke from wood stoves announced that fall had arrived.

There was something spooky about going to work before daylight, but Joanna had a lot to do before the shop opened. There was not much traffic – a lonely patrol car, an empty school bus heading out to begin a rural route, and a delivery truck rumbling along the street. She waved at her paper boy and felt adventurous, being out so early.

Her car scattered a few colorful leaves. When she got out of her car, she heard a flock of Canada geese heading south. The silhouette of their formation glided across the sunrise.

She hummed, her own method of whistling in the dark. Beethoven's *Fifth Symphony* was one of Ben's favorites, and it perked up her courage, adding to the drama

Da, da, da dum-m-m! Da, da, da, dum-m-m!

Joanna spent weeks learning a new piece of music, or months getting ready for a concert. She'd had one evening to prepare for today, but her father's and Ben's support lent her a growing confidence as she unlocked the door.

♫ ♫ ♫

Beth seemed less intimidating than Mrs. Burns, so Joanna was glad she arrived first – but when Beth came in, she was as skittish as a raiding squirrel on Nicholas's favorite bird feeder.

"I can't stay," she said. "I have a big catering job this week."

"Is that good or bad?" Joanna asked, noting the gray circles under Beth's eyes.

"I need the money." She was unusually jittery, almost toppling a tray of rolls as she lifted them to the counter.

"You have to tell me about your trip to Grandfather Mountain, you know."

"I'll tell you all about it later. I promise."

"Like brother, like sister." Joanna felt a tug on her shirt and looked down.

"Benjie saw bear." The musical voice made

her feel ashamed. He clutched a stuffed black bear, obviously acquired at the gift shop at Grandfather Mountain.

"Oh, darling, I didn't mean to neglect you." She knelt down to give him his morning hug. "Did you have a good time? Was Ed fun?"

Benjie nodded and held out the bear for her to admire. His big brown eyes were filled with disbelief as he said, "Ed scared."

"Ed was afraid of the bear?"

"No!" Benjie squealed, breaking into laughter as though she had told the funniest joke of the week. "The bridge! The bridge!"

She turned inquiring eyes to Beth, who explained. "Ed nearly passed out on the bridge."

Joanna was astonished. "Ed would never get on that swinging bridge. Beth, what kind of wondrous transformation are you performing?"

"I didn't know he was afraid of heights! We have to go, Benjie."

She left Joanna with a gaping mouth.

Something is seriously wrong with Beth.

♬ ♬ ♬

Joanna's heart was racing when she went into her spiel with Mrs. Burns. She greeted the woman's arrival with a lighthearted preview of the week.

"We're going to have a reporter from the *Galax Falls News* today, and the radio station is doing a remote broadcast from here tomorrow. A prominent book collector is coming Thursday to check out the books I still have in the closet."

She detected no reaction in Mrs. Burns other than one question. "What did you find out about the value of the book that disappeared?"

"It can't be sold for much without a certificate of authenticity, and Grip Lineberger is the only recognized authority in this area. He's sending me certificates for the other books in the box."

Mrs. Burns nodded.

Joanna plugged in the teapot. "How long did you work for Mr. Henry?"

"Oh, several years, off and on."

"Did he ever talk about the books?"

Mrs. Burns took off her sweater and hung it up. "Mr. Henry didn't talk much about anything. He tried to give me some of those books. I took some old glassware instead. Must have been very foolish of me, I'm beginning to think. I really didn't believe they were of much value."

"I wonder if he had any idea of the fortune he may have left behind."

Mrs. Burns shrugged.

Joanna had begun to think she might be wasting her time with the setup plan, but she elicited a little more response from Lorlene that afternoon.

"Where do you keep the books?" the girl asked.

"In the back closet. They're the ones Mr. Benenson wanted to buy, until we found out how valuable they are. Mr. Lineberger is sending me the certificates of authenticity, which should be here by Wednesday. It's almost impossible to sell an antique book for an appreciable amount without a certificate. A buyer is coming to get them on Thursday."

"You say a reporter is coming here?"

Lorlene shook her blonde hair and fluffed it out with her fingers.

"The radio station is going to broadcast from here tomorrow, and a newspaper reporter is coming today. If you come straight to work from school, I'll try to hold her up so you can have your picture taken for the paper. By the way, the manuscript is under that box under the counter, in case I'm not here when one of them comes."

Lorlene was as interested as a hungry cat at a fish market.

"Could I see it?" she asked.

"I guess . . . " Joanna hesitated. "We'll have to be careful with it."

Grip had explained, in detail, how to give ordinary pages an aged yellow look. Joanna pulled out the box and put on white gloves just as she saw Grip do. The copy of the manuscript was most authentic looking.

"Why are you wearing the gloves?" Lorlene asked.

Joanna explained that old paper was very fragile.

"Wow! What could this be worth?"

"I'm not sure. Mr. Lineberger thinks it could be in the thousands. Perhaps much more. He's consulting experts now."

Lorlene returned to Mrs. Burns. "See, Mom, I told you the old man was loaded. I knew you should have married him."

"I'll be very relieved to have the books gone on Thursday," Joanna confessed.

Customers arrived just as the phone rang, and Joanna would never learn what Mrs. Burns' response would have been about marrying Mr. Henry. The call was from Beth, who wanted to speak to Lorlene.

"Hope you're okay," Joanna said. "We're about to run out of your pastries. We'll sell every roll today."

She took the teapot from Lorlene so she could talk on the phone, and went to serve the table. She was disappointed that Beth wanted to talk to Lorlene instead of her. What could those two possibly have in common?

♫

♫

Chapter Twenty

Reporters were no strangers to Joanna while she was in high school. When she began to win music competitions, the local newspaper started a file on her. The editor showed it to her once, and it was a fat, hefty folder. "You're our town's greatest celebrity," he said.

In her senior year she won the talent award in the state Junior Miss Pageant and was a finalist in a national composition award. Newspaper interviews were usually conducted in her home or at a church, where the photographers could get pictures of her at the organ.

Miss Pansy Zegras, knowledgeable and friendly, was a close friend of her mother, and a musician herself. Joanna remembered her interviews more as visits with a friend than as stressful prodding by a stranger.

Miss Zegras had retired, however, and a young reporter stood before her counter now, wearing a miniskirt and tight black sweater. Her name was Allie Ducker. She looked bored and not especially gifted.

"So what do you want me to say?" she asked.

Joanna did not expect to be responsible for the interview. She was at a total loss.

"I . . . I thought . . . that you wanted a story about the manuscript and antique books."

"Okay. Do you own this shop? Do you have any coffee?"

Joanna served her a cup of coffee, but she was not about to set the manuscript on the table near the coffee even if it wasn't the real thing. She told the young woman, "An antique expert in Winston-Salem thinks we have an original copy of one of O. Henry's unpublished stories."

"Wasn't he some kind of sports reporter?"

"He was a famous short-story writer."

Allie Ducker yawned. "You know, those cinnamon rolls smell delicious."

Joanna served her a roll.

Mrs. Burns came into the shop through the front door. "Hi, Allie. I was hoping you would come this afternoon and get a picture of Lorlene."

"Is this where she works? I'll send the photographer back this afternoon. Those cheerleading pictures of her were terrific."

Mrs. Burns, looking pleased, asked, "Did you know that the manuscript we're talking about could be worth thousands of dollars?"

Allie sat up and straightened her skirt. "Honest? You know, you could buy a real fancy sports car with money like that."

♫ ♫ ♫

The morning mail brought a copy of the *Winston-Salem Journal,* which Joanna spread across the counter. Their enthusiastic and skillful reporter's story featured Grip, and had a photograph of him in his shop examining one of the books. The headline announced:

RARE FIND COULD NET THOUSANDS

She folded the paper carefully to display it on the counter.

The radio reporter, Don Sinclair, appeared promptly at one-thirty to prepare for a two-o'clock remote feature. As energetic and friendly as a puppy, he put Joanna at ease immediately. He read the *Journal* story, then expressed a genuine interest in the manuscript and books she brought out to show him. He seemed to appreciate rare books.

"I remember hearing you in concert once in Raleigh," he said as he set up his mike, "and I love to hear you play at church when I'm in town. At one time I was in the choir there, you know, but I'm on the road most weekends now."

Joanna liked him.

"I love your background music. Let's play that up at the beginning. I'd like to start by speaking to some of your customers. You girls won't mind, will you?" He flashed an engaging smile to three white-haired women who giggled like schoolgirls.

Joanna had called several of her favorite customers, and they were arriving to participate in the show. Two of them were artists who regularly displayed work in the shop. All the tables were filled with friends and Joanna felt grateful for their support. She also had Beth bake a large sheet cake for the occasion. She hoped that her dad would feel up to having Mrs. Campbell drive him to the party.

"I've done a little research," Don said, which let her know that he had prepared for the interview.

"I know that Mr. Lineberger thinks the manuscript is genuine. I called him, and he was excited about it. O. Henry has always been a favorite of mine. Anyway, how did you come to own the manuscript?"

She told him all about buying the shop from Mr. Henry.

"Oh, yes, I remember Mr. Henry. I bought a book from him once. Maybe I'd better check to see if it's valuable. Wouldn't that take the cake? You say these are first editions? Cool."

Mr. Don Sinclair, Joanna thought, *you are one bright spot in an otherwise dreary day.* She was confident that when the show was over, the thief would be itching to get his or her hands on the manuscript.

Just before two o'clock Don checked in with his station and did a quick rehearsal of his introduction. He tightened his tie, straightened it, and put on his suit jacket. "You ready?" he asked Joanna.

Her stereo provided background music for his lead-in. His voice was as smooth as melted chocolate. "Ladies and gentlemen, today *The High Country Street Talker* comes to you live from The Gilded Teapot in downtown Galax Falls."

He motioned to Joanna, and she lowered the volume on the stereo. "We're here because of a remarkable and fascinating discovery, but before I tell you about that, I want to chat with a few lovely ladies who are enjoying tea and cake here in the tea room. Umm-m . . . smell that tea and cake! You must specialize in exotic herbal teas. Save me a slice of that cake, please."

In a deep, friendly voice he said, "Hello, Mrs. Burns." He explained to Radioland that he was speaking to the shop owner's assistant, and Mrs. Burns bustled with efficiency and importance, cutting cake and pouring tea as though it were the White House.

Don carried his mike to the tables for small talk, and by the time the show was in full swing, he had become the new heartthrob for a dozen of the mountains's finest ladies. Then he meandered back to the counter, where Joanna had set out the manuscript.

"Anyone who has read *The Gift of the Magi* will be delighted to learn that O. Henry, also known as William Sydney Porter, may have left a special gift for a Galax Falls lady. Unlike the desperadoes in *The Ransom of Red Chief*, Joanna Jerome is thrilled by her find."

As he began a lively and humorous interview, his exuberance made her forget the microphone. The man was masterfully skilled in his vocation. He read from the list of books that Joanna had prepared for him. "Some of these are undoubtedly destined for museum libraries, but most will be cherished by private collectors who simply love good books."

He continued with an interesting discussion about rare and expensive books, then paused. "I have to slip on cotton gloves, if you'll hold the mike, Miss Jerome. It's important to wear gloves to protect the manuscript's fragile paper when I touch it . . . oh, oh! The gloves are too small. I have big hands, Miss Jerome. In fact, I'm a big man. You'll have to turn the pages for me and show me the manuscript."

There was muffled laughter from the ladies at the tables. "I found out recently that there are methods now to take the acid out of old books and papers. Did you know that? I'm sure you'll have this preserved by an expert, right?"

He held the microphone close to the manuscript so that his listeners could hear the ruffling of the paper. "'The Lackluster Lover.' Certainly sounds like an O. Henry title. Have you learned yet if it is truly an unpublished work?"

Joanna told everything she knew about the manuscript, just as Grip had explained it to her.

Several minutes later Don said, "Ladies and gentlemen, I see the renowned criminal lawyer, Nicholas Jerome, arriving. Mr. Jerome . . . !" He moved across the shop to greet Nicholas.

"Sir, if you had represented O. Henry, he would never have gone to the penitentiary on embezzlement charges, would he?"

"Absolutely not, Don, if he wasn't guilty."

"Are you excited about this manuscript?"

Nicholas chuckled and winked at Joanna. "Of course – and I think my daughter will invest the money wisely."

Don laughed. "How about that? And there you have the exclusive story, ladies and gentlemen, from *High Country Street Talker* live at The Gilded Teapot."

♫ ♫ ♫

How could anyone become so hungry to hear a voice that she hears nearly every day? Joanna wondered as she waited for Ben's nightly call.

When it rang, she grabbed the phone.

"Hello, Joanna Jerome. How'd it go with the reporters?"

"Quite a day. Ben, I wish you'd been there. The newspaper reporter was a dead loss, but the radio guy was terrific. I think we've got a setup that no honest burglar can resist."

He laughed. "I hope we have a self-respecting thief who knows a good deal when he sees it."

"Even Dad came, but he was so worn out afterward that it scared me."

"He mustn't push himself . . . though I don't know how we can stop him."

She heard the clock chiming in the living room. She counted eleven rings. "Not any more than we can stop you from pushing yourself, darling. You are working too many hours."

He sounded weary. "I still have papers to correct, but I'm okay. We do what we have to do."

She nodded in the dark. "I know."

"Did Beth show up?"

"No – and she didn't want any mention of her catering business."

There was a long pause before he said, "I'm worried, honey. She's not herself lately. Something's wrong."

"Maybe she's in love."

His chuckling made her smile.

"Love doesn't make me unhappy and scared," he said.

"Me, either."

"I hate leaving her alone. If I hadn't agreed to sing the solo in the anthem, I wouldn't go to choir practice tomorrow night."

"Ben, I need you! You have to! I've made a point of telling everyone the books would be gone on Thursday. We have set the trap for Wednesday night."

"I won't let you down, sweetheart. I'll pick you up at seven-fifteen."

"Thanks. Sweet dreams, darling. I love you."

"I love you too – but I'm not sure I'll get enough sleep to dream tonight."

She said one final prayer that night. *Please don't let the thief be Beth.*

♫

♫

Chapter Twenty-One

"If I didn't know better," Ben said as they were pulling away from Joanna's house, "I'd think Beth was trying to get rid of me this evening."

"If everything goes well, we'll all feel better when this night is over."

"Did you tell Mr. Hughes about the pager?"

She nodded. "He knows that we have to leave when it beeps."

Joanna's greatest concern was about the one person she hoped they would not find in the shop.

What if she has Benjie with her?

The pager sounded just as choir practice was over. Ben and Joanna slipped quickly out of the church.

"I'm glad Dad could get Barry Jones for surveillance." Her heart raced as they sped down Main Street in the silent night, passed the shop, turned left, and coasted into the alley behind it. Parked next to the shop door was a car that Joanna didn't recognize. "That's not Mrs. Burns' car," she said, her throat dry.

They saw that Barry Jones had parked his car to block the exit at the far end of the alley. Ben turned his car accordingly, blocking their end. Barry leaned into their car and whispered, "Two suspects. One a tall male. The woman is small, young, and blonde as far as I could tell in the moonlight."

"Let us go in first," Ben said. There was an unexpected pleading in his voice, and Joanna realized his great dread of what he was facing.

The darkness was sinister. Joanna had not realized the buildings were so tall or that the alley was so narrow. Each sound bounced off the hard brick and concrete walls like popping ping-pong balls. All sense of adventure fled. *Whoever the thief is, it's someone I've known, and trusted well enough to welcome into my shop.*

As they crept along the alley, she was repulsed by the furtiveness. "Why can't we just march in, turn on the lights, and call the police?" she asked.

"They might have weapons," Barry responded.

A glacial chill gripped Joanna. She wanted to suggest they forget the whole episode and all go home. Every footstep seemed to echo down the damp, dark, concrete canyon.

Ben whispered, "I wish you'd wait outside."

"No way." Her mouth felt gauze-lined.

Quietly Ben unlocked the door and hunched his shoulders against it to ease it open. They froze at the sound of the metallic creak.

Why didn't I think to oil the hinges?

Slowly Ben shoved the door until there was enough space for them to slip inside. They took a moment to orient themselves. The night light in the showroom produced only an anemic glow. The diluted streetlights from Main Street heightened the shadow of the front counter.

A slender streak of light marked the bottom of the closed door to the smaller storeroom. They heard someone stirring in there.

"Stay behind me," Ben said.

They took a step forward. Then Ben stopped and held back his hand to halt her. Joanna heard him take a deep breath before he deviated from their plans.

"Beth?" he asked aloud, his voice trembling.

Joanna's heart sank. *Did he see his sister?*

For a split second there was absolute silence. Then the light under the door disappeared, and the storeroom door slammed back against the wall as the thief sought escape. Joanna jumped back to the door and switched on the overhead lights.

Ben had thrown a body block, shoving his shoulder into the mid-section of a fleeing man. He bounced the intruder off the wall, causing him to hit the floor face down. Barry came in just as Ben put a hammerlock on the stranger.

"Ben, you must be an old football player," he said with a chuckle.

Joanna saw a pinlight beam brush across the front counter. Silently she moved to the showroom. She switched on the lights just as a blonde head dropped behind the counter.

"What are you doing here?" she demanded, stepping around the counter to confront the young woman crouching in the shadows.

"I forgot my purse," Lorlene said defiantly.

Joanna let the pent-up air out of her lungs in a slow, grateful release.

Lorlene stood up, clutching the manuscript box to her breast, and made a beeline for the back door, her hard heels pounding the wood floor like a jackhammer. Barry blocked her escape.

Lorlene glared at the man on the floor. "Why didn't you use your gun, birdbrain?"

"I didn't bring the gun in." The man on the floor craned his head to the side to look up at them. His black windbreaker was pulled up from his jeans, so Barry must have already searched him.

She spat out her disgust with one word. "Idiot."

"I'm not dumb enough to use a gun breaking and entering."

"Smarter than I thought," Barry said.

Lorlene leaned against the wall, breathing hard. "The manuscript should belong to my mom."

Suddenly Joanna felt giddy. "Why, Lorlene, you're welcome to that copy of the story."

The young woman's mouth dropped open, and she stared at Joanna in confusion.

"The original is in New York with a dealer – but you're welcome to this copy. It'll make an interesting conversation piece in your prison cell."

Lorlene slung the box at Joanna. She snarled her contempt, and in a sudden rage jumped around the room, stomping on the yellow pages that she had strewn across the floor, twisting her foot on O. Henry's *Lackluster Lover*.

"You and your big ideas," the man on the floor said.

"They won't blow the whistle on us." Lorlene sneered at Ben. "We can implicate your sister."

Ben's mouth dropped open, and his eyes widened. "What are you talking about?"

"We used her key to get in, and the gun that Al left in the car belongs to her."

"I don't believe it." Ben sounded sick.

"Yeah," Al said, trying to sit up. "The gun belongs to her. She asked me to get it for her."

"You wouldn't dare turn us in," Lorlene said, "because your cute little sister bought a stolen gun from Al. She'll finish paying for it Friday."

"She won't want it," Ben responded, "but you two will need all the help you can get. Make the call, Barry."

"I did. Called from the car phone. Backup's on the way."

"No!" Lorlene wailed. "You can't do this to us!"

"Just watch us," Joanna said.

"My mother will die!"

"I'm sorry about that. I'll talk with my father before making a decision about pressing charges – meanwhile, I'd suggest you give some thought before trying to implicate an innocent person."

"Okay! Okay! I stole her keys. She doesn't know I took them." Lorlene seemed startled by her own confession. "She *did* want to buy the gun though. She begged Al to get it for her."

"But she didn't take delivery on it," Barry reminded them.

"She will. On Friday."

"Over my dead body," Ben said.

Lorlene shrugged. "However you want it. Doesn't matter to me."

♫

♫

Chapter Twenty-Two

Beth did not want Ben to leave her to go to choir practice. She hated being alone in the evenings and had been especially apprehensive since Sunday, but tonight she was more keyed up than usual.

I should have told Ben about the phone call. On the other hand, she needed him gone when Lorlene came. After tonight she wouldn't be so afraid.

"Take care of your mother, Benjie." Ben kissed Beth lightly on the cheek. "I won't be long. If you need anything, call Ed – or Nicholas."

She raised her eyebrows. "Yeah. Call Nicholas. What could he do?"

"You might be surprised what Nicholas can do. I checked the back door. Everything's locked up."

After he left, Beth looked at the flowers Ed had sent. *For saving my life,* he wrote.

She couldn't call Ed. Since Saturday she had hardly slept, worrying about their relationship. He represented a different world from hers; she couldn't drag him down to her level.

She was also angry at him. He could no more understand her fears than he could walk across the swinging bridge. She remembered the evening she asked him to get her a gun permit. He didn't have the vaguest idea of the dark side of life she had known.

He would take care of her, he said. He would call the authorities. *Big deal. What could the telephone authorities do to protect Benjie?*

The cops probably wouldn't help her either; she didn't want to become involved with them. What she needed was a gun. She was determined to get it.

When she went to the window and checked the street, she froze, every nerve in her body taut. A man was lurking at the corner, partially concealed by the telephone pole, just as he was last night and Sunday night. *Why didn't I tell Ben?*

She wished she had let him know about the Sunday phone call – but if Ben thought they were in danger, he might pull up stakes and move again. She couldn't face another move, not away from Galax Falls.

She jerked the curtains shut, lifted Benjie from his highchair, and hurried from room to room, double-checking window latches and pulling shades.

She checked her watch. Lorlene promised to come before eight. Even though Beth had never held a gun, if desperation drove her, she knew she would manage to use it if she had to.

"Time for your bath, Benjie boy."

♫ ♫ ♫

With Benjie tucked into bed, Beth returned to the window. The man was gone from the corner. She sighed, relieved.

Then she saw a movement under the big oak tree in the yard. The muscles in her throat constricted. The streetlight backlit the line of his shoulders and provided a moving shadow as he stirred under the tree.

Her heart seemed to quit beating, and ice flowed through every vein in her body. The man had moved closer to the house. *Was it Jake's brother Archer?* He wore a coat and hat so she couldn't make out any details that might identify him.

Ben wouldn't be home before eight-thirty or nine, even later if he and Joanna went out for dessert after choir practice as they usually did.

She was scarcely aware of picking up the phone and dialing. "Ed . . . Ed, I'm scared."

"Why, honey?"

"There's a man out in our yard."

His voice was irritatingly calm and condescending as he said, "You don't need to worry . . ."

"Maybe *you* don't, but *I* do."

She slammed down the phone. She was frightened out of her wits, and Ed didn't understand. Ben had left her alone. Lorlene had promised her a gun and failed to deliver.

She tiptoed to the bedroom to check on Benjie. His crib was wedged between her bed and the window in the small room. He was sleeping soundly on his stomach, his right arm wrapped around his new bear, his hair fanned out across his forehead. He looked peaceful and secure.

Beth wanted to pick him up and clutch him to her heart. He was her life – she would fight the world for him. She could not, *would* not let them take him. She'd shoot a kidnapper with no remorse at all.

She went back to the kitchen but knew she couldn't possibly keep to her baking schedule now. She was so weak with worry that she couldn't pick up a baking sheet.

She had innocently presumed they would be safe after Jake was sentenced to fifty years in prison for drug trafficking. She had no way of knowing that her ex-husband's brother would take up the harassment. *Will Benjie and I ever be safe?*

She turned off the lights, slipped to the window, and pulled back the curtain. The man was still there, lingering surreptitiously under the dark tree. She had never felt so alone or frightened.

On Sunday the stranger's voice had told her they were coming to get Benjie. She could tell the call came from a cell phone, making it difficult to trace.

A car came slowly down the street. Its lights swept across the yard as it pulled into the driveway. Beth knew from the sound that it was not Ben's car. It moved noiselessly, and she guessed the driver had turned off the engine, to arrive quietly. There was an eerie silence outside.

She dropped the curtain and frantically searched for a weapon. She pulled a knife from the block on the counter, then, doubting her strength to use it, replaced it. She rummaged through the tool drawer, picked up a hammer, then moved soundlessly through the dark house to the front door.

She heard a car door close quietly.

Beth had adapted to the hideousness of a violent marriage, but she did not have a child to protect then. She was forced to endure beatings herself, but she would die to save Benjie.

She knew she should push furniture to the door to form a blockade, but she was too petrified to manage it. She leaned her head against the door and felt the terror climbing up her spine as she heard two men whispering to each other.

God, she prayed, *I'll kill them if they try to take Benjie.* She might get one attacker with the hammer, but then – *How will I fight the other one?*

The only advantage she had on her side was surprise. She moved a footstool next to the door and stood on it. She raised the hammer.

Oh, God . . . help me!

She heard footsteps moving quickly across the porch, and someone rattled the doorknob. She quit breathing.

"Let me in."

There was a sharp knocking on the door. Beth remained frozen. There was such a roar in her ears from her thumping heart that for a minute she could not hear the words clearly.

"Beth . . . let me in. Beth!"

Slowly she lowered the hammer and stepped down from the stool. She wasn't sure she could trust the muffled sound from the other side of the door. "No." Her teeth chattered. "I'm afraid."

"You must trust me. Beth, I can explain about the man. He's a detective – one of our men. Beth, open the door. Call Nicholas to verify what I'm saying. He hired him!"

She remained paralyzed by fear. Then the floor in the hallway creaked, and she whirled around to face a movement in the hall doorway.

"Mommy, me wanna see Ed."

Beth stared at her son. All the air in her lungs rushed out, and she folded forward, dropping the hammer to the floor. She stumbled to the door, dragging her feet, unable to hurry. Her hands shook violently as she pulled back the deadbolt lock.

"Ed!" She fell crying into his arms.

♫

Chapter Twenty-Three

Thursday evening Joanna sat in the police station with her father, Lorlene, Mrs. Burns, and a police officer.

"We don't want to see your daughter go to jail," Nicholas said gently.

Mrs. Burns raised her swollen, red eyes to look at him. "Mr. Jerome, I'm glad that you'll help us."

"I only took the old book to read it," Lorlene said in a subdued voice, "I'll give it back. Anyway, Old Man Henry tried to give the books to my mom."

Nicholas held her eyes with his. "Lorlene, you stole Beth's keys, took cash from the shop, and were prepared to take a great deal more."

"How do you know Beth didn't take the cash? She told me she has a criminal record – "

"Young woman," Nicholas said, his voice harsh, "that has nothing whatever to do with you. Beth begged us not to press charges against you."

Lorlene batted her eyelashes. "She did?"

Joanna said, "She nearly ruined her life by shoplifting. She didn't want that to happen to you."

Lorlene attempted a smile. "What about Al? What'll happen to him?"

"That's up to the district attorney," Nicholas responded. "Luckily, Beth hadn't accepted the gun."

"Whattaya mean? She ordered it. She just didn't have the money to pay for it." Lorlene twisted her hands, wringing them together. "She was gonna pay for it Friday night after some big catering party."

Nicholas leaned over and placed his hand on hers to stop the fidgeting. "I mean," he said firmly, "she *did not accept delivery* of the stolen gun."

"Yes, sir . . ."

He turned to face Mrs. Burns again. "We've discussed it, and Joanna would like you to continue working for her if you want to, but your daughter will have to find a new job."

Lorlene spoke up, incredulous. "You mean I don't have to go to jail?"

"My daughter made that decision, along with the district attorney. I can't promise you're home free, only that we won't press charges – provided you return the book and cash."

Lorlene bit her lip and looked shyly at Joanna. "Thanks." It sounded like a whimper.

♫ ♫ ♫

"You were wonderful, Dad – but you look terribly tired," Joanna said on the way home.

"I *am* tired, honey. Doctor Smith wants me in the hospital for some treatment. Just take me home."

"When did you talk with Doctor Smith?"

"A few days ago. I said we had some unfinished business to take care of first."

"You risked your health because of this fiasco?" Joanna shook her head. "If I had known that, I wouldn't have been so generous with Lorlene."

"I don't have much health to risk – and if you could've seen the shape you and Ben were in Sunday, you'd know I had to stick around to help."

Tears made it difficult to see to drive, but Joanna had learned to control her emotions, at least to hide her pain. "I'll call Andy."

"He's calling me tonight. I'll tell him. I wanted you to know first, so you wouldn't think I was hiding anything from you. Mrs. Campbell can drive me there in the morning, and you can drop by after work."

"No!" Joanna was appalled. "I'll take you to the hospital. I'll close the shop if Mrs. Burns doesn't want to come back."

"Honey, I'd rather you go to work. It's only a minor series of treatments. You need to be there when Beth makes her delivery. Tomorrow's the night of her big party. You and Ben can bring Benjie to see me in the evening."

She drove in silence for several blocks.

"Dad, do you think Lorlene will be all right?"

"No, but I think we've done all we can for her."

"Has Ed talked to you about Beth? He was there with her when Ben got home last night. She had become frightened and called him."

"Ed doesn't have to say anything about Beth," Nicholas said as they pulled into the driveway. "Just look at him. The man is head over heels in love. He was ambushed by Beth and doesn't even know what hit him. I'm expecting a Christmas engagement party."

Joanna set the emergency brake and went around to open his door. She reached in the back seat to get his walker.

"Ed doesn't have to say anything to me any more than you or Ben do," he said, chuckling.

"You sound pleased."

"I'm delighted."

"I hope Andy likes Ben."

"Of course he will. I'll tell him he needs to come home to check him out. He's been talking about coming for a few days anyway."

On Friday evening when they brought Benjie into his hospital room, Nicholas perked up considerably.

"Nick," the child said, "you sick? Want ice cream?"

"Grab that wheelchair, Ben. We'll take this young man to the cafeteria for ice cream!"

"Benjie ride?"

Joanna laughed. "No, Benjie. Nick gets to ride tonight. Do you want to help push the wheelchair?"

"Sure!"

Benjie had grown a lot since he moved to Galax Falls. Joanna remembered how frightened he had been of Nicholas. They were buddies now.

As they ate their treats, Nicholas told them his son was coming for a visit. "Probably tomorrow."

"I'm eager to meet him," Ben said. "I always watch his newscasts when I'm home. He's quite a celebrity. Joanna, did anyone make an audiotape of your radio show? He'd be interested in that."

"As a matter of fact, Don Sinclair sent us a copy today."

"Then why haven't I heard it?"

Nicholas spoke up. "Probably because it sounds like Don might be flirting with your girlfriend." He obviously enjoyed his joke.

♫

♫

Chapter Twenty-Four

Joanna was awakened by Andy, imitating a bugle blowing a rousing army reveille. It was one of her favorite sounds – the way her brother loved to announce his arrival, established in his Boy Scout days.

She grabbed her robe and raced to the kitchen. "Andy! How can you be here so fast? We watched you on the late news last night."

"Hi, Sis." He enfolded her in his arms. "I left immediately after the broadcast."

"You drove all night. Where are Betty and the girls?"

"They couldn't get out of school. We'll be back at Thanksgiving. Betty said to tell you she'll bring the turkey."

"Nonsense. She doesn't have to do that. Let me fix you some coffee and breakfast." She fumbled with the coffee pot. "How long can you stay?"

"Till Monday morning. How is he?"

Joanna hesitated. "His cramps are worse, and he has trouble eating. You know he has already outlived the prognosis. He looks tired but rarely complains. You'd better be prepared. His face looks . . . different. Flat."

"It's the progression of the disease. I've read about that."

"Well, his eyes still sparkle," she said, trying to maintain a brave smile. "Beth and Benjie, our new friends, have breathed fresh life into him."

"So he tells me. I get a daily account of Beth and Benjie – and Ben."

He watched her closely, and she tried not to blush.

People always told Joanna that she and her brother looked enough alike to be twins. Both were tall and brunette, with the unusual dark honey-colored eyes, but their personalities were opposites. She was the quieter one, while Andy was a joker like their father, with his boundless energy.

They sat down at the table.

"I'd forgotten how beautiful the mountains are this time of year. The leaves are as colorful as I've ever seen them," Andy said. "Now. Tell me about this new man in your life. Has he made your move back here endurable?"

"You said you kept up with him."

"I know Dad's viewpoint. I want yours."

"He's the most important thing that ever happened to me." She tried not to gush. "He gave up his doctoral studies to take care of his sister and nephew."

"Sounds like a good match for a wonderful girl who gave up her career to care for her sick father."

"Andy, do you think I would miss being with Dad for anything?"

"I'm sorry I can't be closer."

"He talks an awful lot about Mom lately."

"He and Mom gave us a fine example, didn't

they? I wish my girls could have known her."

They reminisced about their childhood for a few minutes – their pets, trips they took with their parents, their mother's terrible illness and its effect on their father. Then, Andy asked, "How's Ed? Is he still the same stuffy, sonorous barrister, or has Beth changed him, as Dad insists?"

She poured him more coffee. "We'll all have supper together, and you can judge for yourself."

He buttered his toast, grinning. "What's up with this Hercule Poirot stuff Dad's been telling me about?"

She explained about the book and cash disappearing and her desire to set a trap. "Ben and I were afraid that Beth might be involved. Dad was positive that she wasn't. You know he's an uncanny judge of character."

"So how did you set the trap?"

She told about Grip Lineberger calling the newspaper and radio station to promote publicity about the books and manuscript. "I have a tape of the interview with *The High Country Street Talker*."

Andy chortled and nearly choked on his coffee. "The *who*? *What*? Sounds risqué."

They both laughed.

"Then you and Ben played cops-and-robbers. That was dangerous, Sis."

"We hired an off-duty police officer as backup."

"Why didn't you let the police handle it?"

"What? And miss the fun? Actually, we were determined to protect Beth, if she was involved."

Andy folded his napkin. "I don't understand why you suspected her."

"Lots of coincidences. She seemed desperate for money. We didn't know she was trying to buy a stolen gun for protection."

Andy looked shocked. "What in the world would Beth need a gun for?"

Joanna explained about the threats.

"Dad knew all of this?"

"And became deeply involved, of course. He handled the postal threats."

"No wonder he's tired. You've had more adventure in sleepy little Galax Falls than we've had in Atlanta all year. Sounds like a TV mystery." Andy rubbed his jaw. "Jo, I've got to shave and go see Dad."

♬ ♬ ♬

That evening Joanna introduced her brother to Beth, Benjie, and Ben.

"I feel I already know all of you," Andy said. "Dad gives me a daily report."

Beth asked, "Do you talk long-distance with Nick every day?"

"Just about."

Beth looked at the floor. "I haven't talked with my father in months."

"I call Dad one day, and he calls me the next. We've done that since he got sick. I don't get to come see him often."

She sighed. "My father would never call me, not even if I was dying." Her lips quivered, and she reached into her pocket for a tissue. "I'm not sure he would call Ben, either. I guess we were always in the way, or something."

"I rarely talk with my father either," Ed said.

"I don't suppose there are many families as strong as ours," Andy said. "We are grateful, and thank God daily for our dad. I wish you could have known Mother. She was as terrific as Dad is."

When they were seated around the table for dinner, Joanna said, "Andy, you should have been here for Ed's birthday party. Beth catered a meal you wouldn't believe."

"Dad told me about it. By the way, *this* is a fine dinner, Sis."

"It's nothing fancy. I knew we'd want to go to the hospital and wouldn't have time for a big meal."

"Chicken pot pie is fancy for me," Ed said. "I'm trying to learn to heat up soup without scorching it."

"Poor Ed," Beth said.

"Ed scared?" Benjie asked.

Ed delighted the group with a dramatic account of his experience on the swinging bridge at Grandfather Mountain.

Joanna noticed Andy's look of dismay that Ed could so easily poke fun at himself.

Beth said, "Ed, you're exaggerating."

"No, Beth. I thought I was dying."

"Well, Benjie and I weren't about to let you die."

He blushed. "Oh, my." He seemed pleased.

Andy told them that he had seen a news release at the station about the O. Henry manuscript. He wanted to talk his boss into assigning a reporter to do a story about it.

"Please don't," Joanna said. "We've had all the excitement Dad, or the rest of us, can take."

"Speaking of excitement," Beth said, "I didn't know your wonderful father hired a man to protect us at night. I thought the kidnappers were . . ." Glancing at Benjie, she stopped.

Ed spoke up. "You should have seen your sister, Ben. She was standing on a stool beside the door ready to ambush me and splatter my brains with a hammer when I got over there."

"Wow."Andy eyed Beth with admiration. "Do you feel safer now?"

"Yes – and Ed is working on the threatening telephone calls. I was stupid not to tell Ben about them. At least I'm not afraid of an ambush at night."

She used Ed's word, and Joanna noticed that Andy didn't miss the look of adoration she gave the barrister.

♫

♫

Chapter Twenty-Five

Bright fall sunlight splashed through the window, pulling Beth to the door. She needed a break from her baking. "Benjie, wanna go to the lake to feed the ducks?"

"And see Jo-annie?"

She laughed. "We've been there once today, but okay." She quickly made a couple of peanut-butter-and-jelly sandwiches, then stuffed some old bread into a bag for her son to feed to the ducks.

"Benjie walk," he said as she buttoned his sweater.

"Not nine blocks. I have to stop at the store on the way back, so we'll need the stroller to carry the groceries. You push it when we get to town."

Beth walked briskly, not allowing herself to think about kidnap threats and surveillance teams. Conditioned to be wary, she kept a watchful eye on Benjie but focused on her grocery list for the catered Saturday birthday party. Nothing would happen in this sleepy little town in the middle of the afternoon. An ambush would come late at night, when there was no one around to help her.

When they reached Main Street, she lifted Benjie from the stroller to the sidewalk. He stretched to tiptoes to reach the handle. "You ride, Mommy."

"Wish I could, sweetie. Oh, look, there's Joanna across the street. Wave to her."

Suddenly their view was blocked by a gray car that shot around the corner and screeched to a stop beside them. A stranger leaped from the passenger side of the car.

Beth reached for Benjie, but the man slammed the butt of a gun against her head. As she fought the wave of black pain engulfing her, her knees gave way. She sank to the sidewalk, not recognizing that the piercing scream she heard was her own.

The car spun away, pelting the street with loose gravel. Beth lay on the sidewalk, unconscious.

Benjie was gone.

Joanna, returning to her shop from the post office, heard the gut-wrenching scream. For one horrible second, she froze with terror, her eyes helplessly following the gray car as it sped up the street.

She realized what happened just as she heard an explosion of crunching metal and twisting steel. She turned away from the crash and ran to the woman sprawled on the sidewalk. She knelt beside Beth, who had regained consciousness and was fighting to get up.

"Beth, lie still. You're hurt."

"Where's Benjie?" Horror twisted Beth's mouth. She rolled to her knees, and struggled to her feet, pulling on Joanna, swaying, dazed and panic-stricken.

Then, they heard a child's wail.

"Benjie!"

Leaning on each other, they lurched toward

the wreck, nearly a block away. Steam was rising from the gray sedan, jammed between a power pole and the mangled remains of a black car. People emptied from the stores, yelling for police and ambulance, some already using cell phones.

"Benjie!" Beth, gaining a second wind, broke into a full run, with Joanna behind her. Beth pushed through rescuers toward the wrecked BMW. "Benjie! My baby!"

"Your young'un, ma'am?" asked a burly man, who had reached the car first. "Y'all, let the lady through – this here's his mother!"

Several grim-faced men drew back so that she could get to the car. Sirens in the distance grew louder until the noise stabbed through her aching head. She put her hands over her ears.

"Mommy!" Benjie squealed. "Big crash!"

Several pairs of strong arms passed Benjie over to Beth. She gathered him into her arms. Tears and fear subsiding, he draped against her, oblivious to the terror he had been spared. She held him at arm's length to examine his face, his arms, his legs. She caressed him, embracing him close to her heart. "Jo! Call Ben!" They moved away from the car and surge of people.

"Beth, sit down. You're shaking." Joanna took her arm.

"No, I'm all right," Beth said, but her knees buckled, and she sank down to sit on the curb.

"You have a nasty gash, a lump rising on the side of your head – and your leg's bleeding."

"That brute hit me with his gun – but he didn't get away with Benjie!" Beth's voice wavered, and she fought against the tears.

"I'll ask them to call Ben," Joanna said. "We

need to get in touch with Ed, too."

They heard an excited tourist shouting to the police. "I saw the whole thing! It was that driver's fault." She pointed to the black car. "That BMW ran the red light, swerved across the center line, and *deliberately* broadsided the gray car."

Joanna and Beth turned to stare just as Benjie whimpered, "Mommy? Ed's car broke."

Beth's eyes widened in panic. The last trace of color drained from her face, and her lips turned blue. "Oh, no. Ed." She staggered to her feet. "I've got to go to him. Please – here – hold Benjie." Joanna pulled the child into her arms.

Beth pointed at the sidewalk. "Stay *right here* where I can see you. Don't *move!*" She glanced at curious people who formed a circle around them.

Joanna hugged Benjie tightly, and he put his arms around her, snuggling close, his damp little face against her neck. She felt cold chills.

Kidnapped! The threats were real. Benjie was kidnapped right on Main Street . . . She was suddenly weak with nausea, and she sat down on the curb just as Beth had. "Benjie, sweetheart, I love you so much." She squeezed him tightly.

♫ ♫ ♫

Beth doggedly fought a path through the crowd toward Ed's car. The crushed front fender of his BMW trapped one of the kidnappers in the other car. She shuddered at the sight of the getaway car, but she *had* to be sure Ed was alive.

First-responders were prying open Ed's passenger door.

Beth screamed, "Ed!" He did not move.

"Where's that ambulance?" a rescuer shouted.

Beth wriggled between people. When she

was close enough to touch the BMW, she instinctively caressed the glossy polished metal, now torn and jagged. "Please, God, let him be alive!"

She had difficulty comprehending all that happened in an amazingly short time. A lifetime of horror was compressed into seconds of terror. Then she heard Ed's voice. "The child – is he safe?"

"The young'un's fine," one of the rescuers snapped, "No credit to you."

"They were abducting him." His weakened voice trembled with rage.

Beth was scarcely breathing.

A palpible change of attitude among the crowd said that they finally understood. Activity intensified as a police officer spoke into his radio and moved to guard the other driver, still trapped in the gray sedan. Beth saw Ed try to slide toward the door, but he slumped back into his seat, wincing in pain.

"Don't move, Mr. Westmoreland," a rescuer said. "The ambulance is on the way. We'll have to push your car back to get to the other door." The burly man demanded loudly, "Let's get a stretcher here!"

"Yes, sir, Mr. Haynes."

"Ed!" Beth cried.

Ed saw her and whispered, "Benjie?"

"He's okay."

"But you . . . your head . . . "

Beth didn't realize she was hampering the rescue until Mr. Haynes said, "Move back, Ma'am. We need to get him in the ambulance." He added gently, "They'll take care of him. Your head – "

She recognized Mr. Haynes as the man who had changed the flat for them. "I'm fine. Thank you." Now that Ed was in good hands, she limped back to her child.

A police officer blocked her. "Ma'am, you need to get that head wound looked at – "

"Leave me alone!" Beth screamed, dodging around him. "Benjie!" The officer followed.

"Nobody can touch you until you consent, but . . . can you tell me what happened?" he asked.

She couldn't articulate details, the squawking police radio distracted her, the flashing lights hurt her eyes, and all she wanted to do was sit down and press Benjie to her heart forever.

Joanna joined them, carrying the child. She told the officer, "I think she's in shock."

"*My* Mommy – " Benjie leaned far over, stretching for Beth, his eyes wide with shock. Beth gathered him into her arms.

"Where were you, Ma'am?" the officer asked.

The women pointed to the stroller.

"When did you see the car?"

Beth shook her head. "I d – didn't . . . I . . ."

"One suspect got out of the car, but he won't get far. You want to identify the other one for us?"

Her voice wavered. "No – I don't want . . ."

"Here's your brother; I'll talk to him. You can give us a statement later." He turned to Ben. "We only have the one ambulance right now, sir, and they're taking Mr. Westmoreland. They want to monitor him for concussion, so do you think you can get your sister and the boy to the hospital?"

"Of course." Ben drew sister and nephew protectively into his arms. "What happened?"

Beth leaned against him and sobbed. "They jumped me – knocked me down – grabbed Benjie – I couldn't save him, Ben!"

"You were overpowered, honey. You

couldn't do anything."

"Ed stopped them with his car," she whispered, awe in her voice.

"Uncle Ben?" One hand clinging to his mother's neck, Benjie tugged at Ben's shirt with the other.

"There's my buddy! They tell me you're okay, Bud." Ben reached for his nephew, but Benjie recoiled to Beth. "Officer, I hear Ed Westmoreland is the man of the hour. How badly is he hurt?"

"We're taking him to the hospital now. Might have internal injuries and a concussion. Definitely has a broken wrist. Even I can tell that – it's twisted at right angles. Some abrasions. Sure did some fancy driving. Never would have expected it out of him. Stopped that devil without hurting the kid. Someone'll have to identify that other driver."

"I can't guarantee you that I won't strangle him." Ben clenched his jaw.

The policeman nodded grimly. "Sorry we couldn't prevent the attack, sir." He explained to Beth: "We were working with your brother and Mr. Jerome. We were looking for reinforcements by next week. Didn't expect an attempt in broad daylight."

To Ben he said, "You'll need to get your sister and the boy to the emergency room, get her to consent to a checkup. I think they've caught the other suspect, the one who tried to run away. Can you identify the driver for us now?"

Ben nodded and looked at Joanna. "You okay, honey?"

She reached to stroke the child's hair. "I'll get the stroller, and tell Mrs. Burns I'm coming with you."

♫

♫

Chapter Twenty-Six

Beth was staggering, nearly falling. Joanna realized that the girl was more seriously hurt than they first thought. She looked like a frightened little waif, almost unaware of her surroundings, hugging Benjie close. The bruise on the side of her head was red and puffy, and her scraped leg was bleeding again.

She must be suffering from shock. Indeed, they all were. Benjie was kidnapped right in front of them. For the first time Joanna understood Beth's obsession about protecting him. Perhaps they had all hoped she was overreacting when she wanted to get a gun.

Ben found a wheelchair for his sister. Her eyes darted around the emergency room, and she stared vaguely at the receptionist. The contrast between the spunky, vivacious young woman Joanna knew and the drawn, miserable-looking girl in the wheelchair was startling.

Beth stared at the blue uniform of a police officer standing near the reception desk and raised her eyes to him. "I want to see Ed."

He nodded. "I understand."

"Beth, honey," Ben said, sorting through his insurance cards, "they're going to have to check you and Benjie out first."

"No! I have to see Ed." She spoke to the nurse. "Can you tell me where he is?"

"Mr. Westmoreland? They're preparing him for surgery. We'll let you see him as soon as we can, but first we need a doctor to look at that head wound. You have a nasty cut. The baby better be checked, too." She told Ben, "I'll take her."

"Wait!" Beth exclaimed. "Ben, you and Joanna promise me you'll take good care of Benjie. Don't let him out of your sight. Promise me."

They promised.

"Mommy sick?" Benjie quavered as a nurse pushed the wheelchair away down the hall. He threw himself sideways in Joanna's arms, reaching after the vanishing wheelchair. "I want *Mommy*!"

Ben caught the child and gathered him into his embrace. "In a minute, buddy. The doctor needs to make her better."

"Mommy hurt?"

"Yes, son – but not much. She'll come back soon. Let's go with this lady and check you out, too, like Mommy, okay?"

They followed a nurse to a treatment room for Benjie's check-up. Pronounced unhurt, he was released, and the three settled into the waiting room.

Ben sat the little boy on his knees. Benjie twisted so he could confront him directly, then placed a small hand on either side of Ben's face and turned his head so that he could gaze into his eyes. He stared at him with deep creases between his eyebrows. "Ed's car broke," he said.

In spite of the child's earnestness, Ben smiled.

"Yes, but cars can be fixed."

"Why?"

Ben shook his head and said to Joanna, "My friends who have children have warned me about the 'why' stage."

She smiled. "He's a little young for it, but not many two-year-olds have been through what he has."

The little boy persisted. "Benjie in car crash. Bang! Why did they did that?"

Ben sighed. "I suppose I'd better be honest."

He raised the little chin, and a look of tenderness spread across his face. "Benjie, some mean men wanted to take you away from your mommy. Ed crashed into their car so that they couldn't get away. Ed was protecting you. The police have taken the men to jail, where they can't hurt you or your mommy ever again."

"Where's Ed?"

"His hand was hurt in the crash. The doctor is putting a bandage on it, so it will feel better."

Benjie's back stiffened as a police officer walked into the waiting room. He cringed against Ben.

"Hello, son," Officer Harvey said. "I'm glad to see that you're doing okay."

An aide signaled to Ben, and he stood up. "Excuse me," he said to the officer, placing Benjie in Joanna's lap. "The nurse is calling me."

"I'll take Benjie up to see Dad," Joanna said. "He'll be hearing rumors, and I must tell him what happened."

Benjie stared at the policeman's silver badge. He pointed to the gun in the holster. "Shoot Benjie?"

Instead of laughing, the officer squatted down in front of him and spoke quietly, professionally. "No, son. My weapon is to help protect Benjie."

Joanna said, "Officer, I'd rather not answer questions in front of the child. May I talk with you after I've seen my father?"

"Of course, Miss Jerome. We have a bunch of other statements to take. You go see your father first. Is he doing all right?"

"As well as can be expected. Thank you for asking." Joanna asked about Ed, then spoke to Benjie. "Would you like to see Nicholas with me?"

Benjie slid down from her lap. "Sure!" He held up his hand to grasp hers and, after a final stare at the holster, walked bravely past the policeman.

♬ ♬ ♬

Beth felt faint, and sank gratefully into the wheelchair Ben found for her. She hated the smell of an emergency room. It reminded her of the times she had been taken to hospitals after beatings by her ex-husband. The antiseptic scent brought back all the pain. She almost expected to see Jake slinking around a corner, sulking because she needed medical attention, drunkenly harassing the nurses.

She wanted to see Ed. She *had* to see him. But when the nurse rolled her chair away from Ben and Benjie, she was suddenly too tired to protest.

They pushed her into a cold, sterile room. She hoped they would not leave her alone. *What if the kidnappers were brought to the hospital?* She didn't want to see them. "Can my brother stay with me?" she asked.

"Of course. I'll send for him," the nurse said.

When Ben came into the room, Beth broke down, crying. "Ben, where's Benjie? You promised!"

"He's fine. Joanna took him to see Nicholas."

"I can't find out how bad Ed was hurt," she sobbed. "What if they bring Archer here?"

"Then I'll have to stomp him into dust."

She managed a weak smile.

"He won't be here," Ben assured her. "They have him in custody. We don't have to worry about him anymore."

An attendant opened the door.

"Mr. Westmoreland is asking to see Ms. Morgan before he goes to surgery," she told the nurse. "We have him outside. Can she come out into the hall to speak to him?"

Ben didn't wait for the nurse to answer as he maneuvered the wheelchair to the door.

"Ed," Beth whispered, "how bad do you hurt?"

She started to touch his sheet-draped form but drew back her hand. She staggered to her feet and gently laid a hand against his cheek.

"Thank you for saving Benjie."

"I had to." Ed sounded as if he were speaking past a mouthful of cotton. "I didn't get you a gun permit. Is Benjie okay? How is your head?"

"We're fine."

The attendants were already moving the gurney down the hall. Beth followed a step or two, then turned back toward Ben. He took her arm and helped her ease her body down into the wheelchair, favoring the scraped leg. *I feel like I'm a hundred years old.*

"The doctor is ready to see you now," the nurse said.

♫

♫

Chapter Twenty-Seven

In a town the size of Galax Falls, news about the kidnapping and the capture of the criminals spread rapidly. Within hours Ed became the town hero. A police officer had to stand guard outside his room to keep away the reporters and the merely curious.

Joanna couldn't imagine how the media got the news so fast, but Andy tracked her down before she left her father's hospital room.

"What on earth are you people in the mountains mixed up in now?" he asked over the phone.

"How did you find out so quickly?"

"The wire services are hot on the story. I didn't know that Beth's ex was such a big-time hood. We need to move back to Galax Falls to be where the action is."

"Oh, trust me, Andy, you don't want this kind of action."

"You're right. Well, Beth *said* she needed a gun. Hollywood is probably already working on the script. We should ask Ed who he wants to play his character. How's Benjie doing?"

"I'll let him tell you. Benjie, do you remember my brother Andy? We ate dinner with him last week? He wants to say hello to you."

The little boy grinned and held the phone with both hands. "Hello?"

"Benjie! What happened to you?"

"Crash! Bang! Ed's car broke. Nick wants ice cream."

When Joanna took the phone back, Andy was laughing.

"How is Dad handling it all?" he asked.

"I have to go back to the emergency room with Benjie, so I'll let him tell you," she responded, "but, Andy, don't send any reporters here!"

♫ ♫ ♫

Since Benjie had passed his checkup and Beth was in good hands, Ben needed to get back to school. Beth refused to leave the hospital until Ed was out of surgery, so Joanna took Benjie with her. When they walked into the shop, it was crowded and noisy with customers and well-wishers.

Mrs. Burns looked relieved. "Am I glad to see you! Oh, you brought Benjie! Hey, Sweetie." She was flushed with excitement. "This place has been a circus – but I love it."

Holding Benjie on her hip, Joanna greeted her friends. Questions were hurled at her from every direction. "Beth is fine. Ed's having his broken hand set. You can see that Benjamin Morgan here is *wonderful*." She hugged him, closing her eyelids tightly to keep the tears of relief in check.

When the shop cleared out a little, she suggested to Mrs. Burns that they close the shop for the day.

"Why? Then people would just pester you at home. Your brother's been calling, and there have been calls from Greensboro and Winston-Salem. I can handle the customers if you want to stay open – oh, but we're almost out of pastries."

"I'll call Mrs. Campbell. I think she'd be willing to bake a cake or two. Just direct all questions about the accident to the police. Mrs. Burns, what would I do without you?"

"Joanna, I'm glad to be here for you." Her smile showed she meant it.

♬ ♬ ♬

Benjie was having trouble keeping his tired eyes open, so Joanna took him to her house for a nap. When she sat down beside the bed to read to him, fatigue hit her as if someone had dumped a bucket of warm water over her head.

Benjie drifted right to sleep, but she was too tired to move. The enormity of the day's events struck her. *What if the kidnappers had been successful?*

She remembered the panic in Beth's face, then the relief. Another thought now settled in to haunt her, one that had been dancing around in her mind. *Beth, at the age of twenty-two, has a son.*

She felt a longing stir within her as she watched Benjie sleeping. He looked enough like Ben to be his son. Joanna had been caught up with her career and her father's care; she had seldom contemplated motherhood.

Now deep feelings for Ben rose in her, and a warm flush spread across her whole body. She had never been so unmistakably in love, not with anything like the consuming love she felt for Ben. She realized that unconsciously she had been looking for him all her life, and found him in her own home town.

Gratitude filled her, and she breathed a prayer of thanks.

When she had rested for a few minutes and assured herself that Benjie was asleep, Joanna slipped quietly to the den to handle the list of phone calls Mrs. Burns had prepared for her. There was a call from Don Sinclair; she would ignore that one for now. She would save the calls from Greensboro for Ben to return.

The next number on the list had the word *Important* scrawled next to it. Grip Lineberger's message said that he wanted her to return his call as soon as possible. Joanna tried to draw a mental portrait of the funny little man as she listened to the phone ringing.

"Miss Jerome!" He sounded breathless. "What kind of retirement program do you have?"

She had never thought about retirement and was unprepared for the question. "Why?"

"You aren't going to be a rich woman from the sale of these books, but you'll have enough to set up a fine retirement program."

She was surprised by the prices he quoted her. "Unbelievable, Grip. Thanks."

"Ben said you recovered Homer's *Iliad*. I'm prepared to offer you three thousand for it. I want it for my own collection."

She drew a deep breath. "And the manuscript?"

"Precisely the reason I wanted to speak to you. One of the finest auction houses in New York City wants to put a reserve bid on it for thirty thousand dollars. That way it won't sell for less, but it might go for much more. If you are agreeable, we'll negotiate a contract."

"Of course, if you recommend it."

"Hey, my assistant keeps asking me if I met that lawyer with the wrecked BMW."

"He's my father's partner."

"Is he going to be all right?"

"Yes, fine. Did you know the boy he saved is Ben's nephew?"

"You're kidding! Hallelujah, praise the Lord!"

"Amen. Absolutely. And thank you, Grip."

♫ ♫ ♫

"Ed is becoming quite the media luminary," Joanna said to Ben when he came to take them to the hospital.

"He deserves every bit of it. We'll be grateful to him forever."

"Have you spoken to your parents?"

"I called them from the emergency room. I knew they'd hear about it on the news. Know what they asked?"

He sounded miserable.

"I can't imagine," Joanna responded.

"They wanted to know if we have to pay the damage on the lawyer's car."

She felt sorry for him and Beth.

"Ed has collision insurance, but we could pay the damages if we needed to." She told him all about Grip's call, right down to quoting his "Hallelujah, praise the Lord."

"Amen," Ben said.

"That's exactly what I said!"

He raised her chin and stroked her cheek. Joanna felt him trace the contour of her temple and ear with his finger before he leaned down to kiss her tenderly. "Did you enjoy playing mother for the day?" he asked.

"I loved it."

His smile touched her. "Fabulous news from Grip. What will you do with all that money?"

She laughed. "I haven't thought about the money. Maybe you ought to go back to graduate school."

"Joanna Jerome, the money's yours, not mine."

"I'll not marry a man who can't share everything with me."

He seemed unable to speak.

♫

Chapter Twenty-Eight

Beth heard a faint groan and struggled out of her chair to stand beside Ed's bed. Her own breathing marked time with his.

She had been watching the shallow rising of his chest as he inhaled, and the slow relaxing motion as he exhaled, scarcely disturbing the contour of the blanket that covered him. She wanted to touch him, but was daunted by the bulky white cast that extended from his fingers to above his elbow. She started to stroke his forehead but remembered the concussion.

His eyelids fluttered, and when he opened his eyes, she leaned over to kiss his bare shoulder.

"Beth? What are you doing here?"

She bit her lip. "Waiting for you to wake up."

"You should be home, resting." He turned his head to study her bandage. "We're quite a pair," he said with a slight chuckle and closed his eyes again. "What time is it?"

"Almost supper time."

He kept his eyes closed, but a few minutes

later he asked, "Are you still here, sweet one?"

"I'm here, Ed. Do you need anything?"

"If you're here, I have everything I need." He dozed again. As she continued to measure the rise and fall of the blanket, she noticed that his breathing was less shallow. Beth tried not to bend her stiff leg as she sat back down. She remained still, content to keep her vigil at his bedside.

He's a good man. An unfamiliar stirring, in the deepest part of her consciousness, pushed itself to the surface of her mind. When she was with him, she felt like a good woman. With him, the sense of worthlessness she had lived with for twenty-two years evaporated.

She remembered the first time she visited his law office, when she apologized for calling him a horse. He had said, "Beth, you don't need to be ashamed. About anything."

That was the first time in her life that it occurred to her that she didn't need to be ashamed of herself and what she was. Ed made her feel noble.

She remembered his look of admiration when she told him about saving the owl in the fireplace.

"Good for you," he had said. It was a simple statement, but he had leaned across his desk and smiled at her. She had felt a warm flush of pleasure.

"How can you say that you've messed up your life," he had asked on Grandfather Mountain, "when you produced Benjie?"

She recalled the way he bragged so outrageously about the bridge incident. She wasn't accustomed to people bragging about her. Ed accepted her just as she was. She hadn't known that love was a healing balm.

In the beginning she pretended to herself that

what she felt for him was merely a foolish infatuation, hero worship. She simply expected to admire him from afar and have a little fun with it, the big-time lawyer and the penniless single mom. The knowledge that he loved her was an unbelievable gift that she was still trying to comprehend. He didn't make fun of her zany sense of humor. He never made her feel dumb – and he loved her son enough to risk his life. She watched him sleeping, and her heart overflowed.

Ed was very different from Ben and the other men she had known. Ben was laid back, down-to-earth; Ed was smothering in formal dignity. A few months ago she would have been contemptuous and would have delighted in making fun of him.

Haughty. She had thought he was pompous. Perhaps he is just a little arrogant and sure of himself. Nevertheless, she loved him.

She wished she had asked Ben to bring her some clean clothes. The smell of blood on her blouse was nauseating. She didn't even have a hair brush, though it would be difficult to use one if she did. The nurse had washed the blood-crusted wound, but her hair felt stiff and dirty.

She leaned against the bed and closed her eyes. Ed stirred in his sleep, touched her hair, and rested his hand gently on her shoulder. A wonderful assurance took hold of her, and the tension drained from her neck and shoulders. Ed had stopped Archer; the police arrested him. The threat against Benjie was over. It was difficult to conceive of the new splendor of her life.

She heard a wheelchair squeak and looked up to see Nicholas at the door. She stood up and caught the side of the bed to wait out the surge of dizziness that hit her.

Nicholas paused to speak to the guard, quickly pumped his arms, and moved the wheelchair closer to her. "Should you be here?" His face was clouded with concern as he considered her head bandage.

"I don't want to be anyplace else," Beth said. "I want to be with Ed."

A raspy voice floated up to them from the pillow. "She's a glutton for punishment."

Nicholas pressed Beth's hand to his lips. "Sit down, dear." He went around to the other side of the bed. "Ed, are you running a demolition derby?"

"I'm working on it. I just wish I'd been driving a company car. I'll be back to the office soon." Ed's joke fell flat, as did most of his attempts at humor. His voice sounded stronger as he added, "My secretary can handle my work."

Nicholas laughed. "The office can wait, but I'm going crazy trying to get the sequence of events clear in my brain. I'm eager to hear your side of this drama."

Ed fumbled with his control panel, and the head of his bed rose so he could see Nicholas in his wheelchair.

Beth spoke up. "Not too high, Ed." To Nicholas she explained, "He has a concussion." She found his glasses, and he put them on with his left hand. Beth helped adjust them.

"Tell you what I remember," Ed said, his tongue thick. "Everything's a bit fuzzy. I was a couple of blocks away when I saw Benjie pushing the stroller, so I thought I'd drive by and honk on my way to court. Benjie loves my horn. When I saw that – criminal – jump out of a car and grab him . . . what else could

I do? I stopped them. That's all. Simple."

"Sure. Simple." Nicholas shook his head and winked at Beth. "How bad's the hand, Ed?"

"Hasn't hurt since they set it. I broke it when I jammed into the other car. My car stopped, but I didn't. The airbag saved me from serious injury. They insisted on keeping me overnight for observation. I'm fine, just a bit groggy."

"I'm going home tomorrow too," Nicholas said, "so we can go together. You can't drive and don't have a car. You'd better come to the house with me and let Mrs. Campbell take care of both of us. Beth can delight us with her culinary skills – if you're able, dear, with the head wound and bandaged leg."

Ed struggled to sit up. "What happened to your leg, Beth?"

"Ed, lie down. It's okay. I scraped it a bit on the sidewalk."

He sank back down. "I'm sorry. Nicholas, did you know that thug gashed her with his gun?"

Choking with sudden horror, Beth said, "I can't even think about what they were going to do to Benjie." Ed patted her hand, and Nicholas quietly reassured her.

"That hoodlum will be behind bars until Benjie is an old man, honey. You won't ever have to worry about him. Oh, I wish I could be a prosecutor for just that one last case."

Beth's chin jerked up. "You mean we'll have to go through another trial?" She covered her open mouth with both hands, her eyes filled with dismay.

"'We' means Ed and me, and our whole law firm and all the other great friends you've made in Galax Falls. You'll not be alone."

"Nick, Ed . . . you are both so wonderful to

me. Thank God. I'm so glad Benjie and I have you."

"Speaking of Benjie, here he is!" Nicholas said, turning to face the door. "Hello, big shot."

"Is this some kind of convention?" Ben asked.

Joanna exclaimed, "Dad, you gadabout!"

"Hey, Nick," Benjie asked, "want ice cream?"

The room exploded in laughter, and he rushed to his mother's open arms.

♬

♫

Chapter Twenty-Nine

The thunderstorm crashed through a crescendo to its climax, then into diminuendo, and finally marched off to the southeast, leaving a steady rain tapping a repetitive drumbeat on the decks – *plop, plop, pa-plop*. The weather had kept Ben and Nicholas from a Saturday ride around the lake.

In the den, Nicholas pushed the mute button on his remote control, and the blare of the ball game died. Joanna found the atmosphere refreshingly peaceful after the turmoil of the thunder and television. Sitting in the dining room working on her shop account books, until now she had paid little attention to the conversation of the men.

The monotone of her father's voice could have lulled her to sleep but she listened from the next room, enjoying the pleasant cadence – the rhythmic pattern in his speech, even though he was speaking more slowly each day.

"Jo used to be a fine composer. Her mother thought she'd produce some masterpieces, but . . . "

Joanna jerked her chin up. Thoughtfully she laid down her pencil. *How did I continue to work when the room has become so dark?* She stroked her golden medallion as she listened.

She rubbed her eyes and caught a glimpse of herself in the mirror on the china cabinet. She looked tired, and she felt an overwhelming sadness for the fatigue in her father's voice. Treatments in the hospital had not helped.

"Perhaps she'll compose again," Ben said.

"When?"

Nicholas's voice sounded almost sharp. He was becoming uncharacteristically grumpy. "Not while she's running a gift shop and caring for a sick old man," he said. "Talent held hostage too long will dissipate."

"Talent held hostage?" Ben returned. "What are you talking about? Joanna's talent isn't dissipating. Don't you hear her play each Sunday? I tell you, sir, the first time I heard her play, she struck a golden chord in my heart."

Joanna smiled and wondered if Ben was aware she was wearing the medallion today.

For a moment the house was stuffy with silence. The rain was petering out, but the humidity clung to everyone like a damp embrace.

Joanna heard a catch in her father's voice. "Thanks for reminding me, son, but I want much more for her. She needs to soar, to give back to the world of music some of what God has blessed her with. She needs time to compose and practice."

"I wish I knew what to tell you, Nicholas."

"I'll tell you what I want to hear." His voice sounded rejuvenated, and Joanna smiled.

Ben chuckled. "So what's new? You usually do. Tell me."

Joanna cherished the easy camaraderie between the two men she loved. She imagined Ben leaning forward, eager to please, with his wondrous gift for listening. She heard the kindness in his voice, the encouragement that would lift her father's spirits, and her heart was filled with gratitude.

"I want to know that you are going back to graduate school, that you will finish that Ph.D., and that Joanna is working on her music. She needs the stimulus of a university campus."

Joanna stood up and edged to the doorway. She didn't want to interrupt the dialogue.

Nicholas said calmly, "Hospice is coming this week. The next few months are going to be difficult for Jo. I'm glad you're here, Ben, but I want her to have a goal, a dream, to fortify and sustain her during this transition."

"So you want me to catch her a rainbow."

Ben glanced at Joanna and acknowledged her with a slight nod.

"I want you both to get your lives back on track."

Ben raised his eyes to study Joanna. "I've never been more on track in my life than since I found Joanna," he said with more emotion than she had heard him express. "I love your daughter with all my being. With Beth's new life I can begin to reconsider my own options – but I gave up my fellowship."

Nicholas shifted impatiently in his wheelchair. "Bah! There are other programs, and other schools."

Ben studied the floor. Joanna saw a struggle going on by the way he leaned over, clasped his hands, and dropped them between his knees. His forehead puckered, causing deep ridges that gave him the appearance of a much older man. Finally he pressed his lips together and looked at Nicholas.

Joanna saw the grim line of his mouth, and her heart froze. There was a formidable, stubborn expression in his eyes. "I suspect there are," he said, his lips quivering and reshaping into a broad smile. "I suspect there are. I'll check into it."

"Thanks, Ben. I give you and Joanna Psalm 37: 3 and 4: 'Trust in the Lord, and do good. Delight yourselves in the Lord and he will give you the desires of your heart.' Now, I'll face my departure in peace."

Joanna slipped into the room and knelt beside her father's wheelchair. He placed his hand over hers as she gripped his armrest.

"Death is nothing to fear," he said firmly, "when you have an understanding about your full insurance policy and love for those dear ones who have gone on before – like your precious mother, Jo. I have no dread, only a great anticipation."

Ben stood and moved behind Joanna. He placed one hand on her shoulder and one on Nicholas's. "Amen." His voice was husky.

The moment wrapped about them like a tender caress binding them to a priceless memory saved forever, like a photograph in the family album.

Outside, a thin pink cirrus cloud spread across the horizon, pulling the blue of the cleared sky and a glorious rainbow across the mountains. The sun was dispelling the storm, touching rain-drenched trees, igniting diamond-like sparkles.

Suddenly Nicholas threw back his arms and shook the afghan from his knees. "Enough! Now let's plan an engagement party." He looked up and noticed Joanna's look of consternation. "For Ed and Beth!"

♫

♫

Chapter Thirty

Joanna hoped she wouldn't resent customers today. All she wanted was a few quiet hours to work alone. Days of installing new caretakers for her father and changing her schedule to allow more time at home had drained her emotionally and physically.

She had given Mrs. Burns the day off, desperate for some time by herself. After today Mrs. Burns would be in charge of the shop most of the time, with Beth helping for several hours during the mornings.

Cindy Pacileo came early, loaded down with boxes of her ceramic work. "Your boxes weigh more than you do," Joanna joked. Nicholas had enjoyed the small table fountain she had designed for his reading table as a gift, but Joanna had sold several similar ones.

"I have the surprise Beth ordered for Ed," she said and unwrapped a perfect little screech owl. "She's really crazy about that guy, isn't she?" She held the bird in her hand. "Even life-size, these are quite small."

Cindy ran her hand through her short graying red hair and wondered, "Were you surprised when Ed wrecked his prized BMW to stop the kidnappers?"

"Somehow," Joanna said and laughed, "nothing about Ed and Beth surprises me anymore. And Benjie just adores Ed – has since the first day he saw him. That was a hoot!"

"Tell me about it," Cindy begged as she unwrapped her other packages. "It was a hoot?"

Joanna didn't have the time, but couldn't resist telling about Benjie hanging on to Ed's leg. "Benjie is irresistible." Cindy stayed for a second cup of tea.

Claude Schneider and his wife, Elizabeth, arrived from Jonas Ridge just before noon. He brought a new pastel painting – a woven basket filled with red and green apples.

"They look good enough to eat, and I think I can smell them," Joanna said.

"I doubt they would be very tasty." He brushed his hand down his long, gray beard.

Elizabeth said, "I believe it is some of your tea you are smelling – and what a wonderful aroma of muffins! Let's take time for a treat, Claude."

"What did Lila bring to replace the picture you sold?" the artist asked.

Joanna wished Benjie was there to meet Claude and Elizabeth. He could pass for a slender Santa Claus, except she would have to explain the black patch that hid his blind eye. How a man with one eye could produce such exquisite art, Joanna would never know.

She pointed to a watercolor on the wall entitled: "First Day of School."

Claude walked over to it. "That's a study of the old school in Roan Mountain. She started it on a field trip in my class. I said to put the children in old fashioned clothes."

After the Schneiders left, business was mercifully slack, and Joanna was able to work on her orders for new merchandise. Her solitude was shattered when the door flew open with such gusto that she spun around from the cash register in alarm.

♫ ♫ ♫

If the only image she had of Beth had been the one she projected in the hospital emergency room, Joanna wouldn't have recognized the young woman standing in the doorway of the shop.

"Joanna," she sputtered, her face flushed with excitement, "I need you to help me!" Beth stood poised at the doorway with all the radiance and presence of a reigning queen, in spite of her blue jeans and tee shirt. She shimmered with pleasure, filling the shop with a sense of expectancy.

"How?" It was the only word that came to mind. *Help? Beth has the world by a string.*

Benjie broke away from his mother and raced to Joanna. "He refuses to ride in the stroller anymore," Beth explained, "even on the long walk from the house."

"Benjie big," the child said.

"You are, sweetheart." Joanna pretended to have trouble lifting him. "How can I help you, Beth?"

"Ed just called. We're going to meet his parents this weekend, and I don't have any decent clothes to wear. You've got to help me with some shopping. I can't wear these to meet Ed's mother!" She spread out her hands and looked down at her casual attire, shuddering. "She'd faint dead away. I've seen pictures of her. She always dresses like she was going to church. Ed says I need to look for honeymoon clothes, too, but we don't need to do that today." She was blushing, her lips trembled, and she began to cry.

"Beth, honey . . . why are you crying?"

"I'm so happy. Remember that first time in here when I was so cruel to Ed? He should have hated me. Who would've ever thought he'd fall in love with me?"

Joanna led Benjie to a table and sat down. He had, as was his custom, accepted one cookie for each hand from the tray she held out to him. Luckily, he paid no attention to his mother's tears.

"My dad did, for one. He said you were perfect for Ed from the very beginning."

Wonder washed Beth's face. "Your dad – Nicholas predicted this?"

"He said you were just what Ed needed."

Beth brushed away the tears and giggled. "Me?

Remember how Ed acted when I called him a 'handsome devil'?"

"I remember how angry I was, because I thought you were being unkind to him."

Benjie crawled up into Joanna's lap. Beth slid into a chair, kicked off her sandals, and stretched out her legs.

"We're going to choose an engagement ring in Charlotte too. I'm a little terrified, to tell you the truth." She twisted her feet and curled her toes, straightened them, and rattled on, oblivious to her nervous mannerisms. "If Ed's brother calls him 'Owl' in front of me, I'll smack him a good one." She stuck out her chin and drew down her eyebrows with exaggerated anger.

"Oh, that would endear you to the entire family." Joanna laughed so hard, she had trouble holding Benjie. "It's been a dull morning, and I'd like to take a break. When do we need to plan this shopping expedition?"

"Whenever you can get off to go with me. Ben can babysit tonight. He said to tell you he'll take Benjie over to check on Nicholas."

Joanna nodded. "Let's go when I close up."

Beth looked worried. "I can't run around town dressed like this after we're married. Oh, Joanna, how will I ever work up enough polish not to embarrass Ed with his friends?"

Joanna leaned across the table and gripped her wrist. "Now, just a minute, young lady. Did Ed ask you to change?"

"No! But I want to be an asset to him." Beth pushed her short hair back over her ear.

"Ed fell in love with you just the way you are, and we'd all be disappointed if you changed much. We don't want you to be anyone except Beth."

"But I look so – "

"Refreshingly wonderful."

Beth stared at her. The worried look evaporated from her forehead, and she gave a deep sigh and smiled. "No wonder Ben loves you so much."

"And no wonder that Ed loves you. Cindy brought the owl you ordered."

Beth forgot all her worries and fears as she lifted the little gray owl from its box.

♫ ♫ ♫

It had been years since Joanna had so much fun in department stores. She felt as if she were back in high school, giggling over prom dresses. For a little while she was able to push away sad thoughts and found herself thinking wistfully about buying her own wedding trousseau.

Beth's interest in fashion was obviously nonchalant, but tonight Joanna had trouble steering her away from flashy, flamboyant clothes. She made her think of a fellow Junior Miss contestant who wanted everything to be plastered with sequins and rhinestones. Joanna helped her find a simple sheath dress that showed off her tiny figure.

"I don't have much money to spend, but Ben told me to buy anything I needed. I'll buy another blouse and skirt," Beth said when they paused for a light supper. "Your clothes are so elegant, I knew you'd know where to shop."

"I haven't spent much time shopping lately, but my mother had real style and a good eye. She spent lots of time shopping for me. She was petite like you, Beth. We saved her wedding dress, but it's too small for me. Let me talk to Dad . . ."

"I couldn't possibly wear your mother's wedding dress, although it would be a great honor. Ed's already chosen my outfit."

"What?"

Beth raised earnest eyebrows to Joanna. "Don't laugh. Bet you never knew he's so sentimental. He wants me to wear the skirt and blouse I wore at his birthday party. He says that was when he began to fall in love with me."

"Your wedding dress has to be special. Wear that skirt and blouse on your honeymoon, but let's shop for a truly elegant dress – or, of course, if you change your mind, you can always try on my mother's gown."

"I'll discuss it with Ben." Her voice dropped, and she frowned. "You must miss your mother very much. I don't remember ever shopping with mine. Just think, Joanna. We're going to be sisters!"

"One good reason to marry Ben."

While looking at shoes, Beth startled her by asking, "Why didn't you marry Ed? I know he's crazy about you and Nicholas."

Joanna was pensive for a few moments. "Yes, he thought of us as a unit, but that was before he met you. I've waited all my life for Ben. Ed will make a great brother-in-law, and he loves you."

"Do you remember that first dinner at your house? Nick called us a family. I thought it was a fantasy, but – "

"We *are* a family. We love each other, and we care for each other. When are you taking Ed to meet your folks?"

"They aren't particularly interested. Ben keeps inviting them to come up here to visit. When do you think you'll be married?"

"It's not a happy time to be preparing for a

wedding at my house."

"I'm sorry." Beth slapped her hand across her mouth. "I'm so excited about my own wedding, I want everyone else to be just as happy."

"It's okay. Ben reminds me that we'll have the rest of our lives together. I must concentrate on Dad now."

"Perhaps Ed and I ought to wait."

"No. Dad's counting on attending your wedding. Ed is like a son to him – and Benjie is like the grandson he'll never know."

Joanna became self-conscious as Beth studied her face, gazing at her with a somber expression.

"I don't want to remind you of Nick's illness, but Ed said that if he's too sick to attend our wedding at the church, perhaps we could be married at your house."

"We would be honored."

There was a catch in Beth's voice when she said, "Getting to know Nicholas has been a great blessing. He's certainly Ed's hero."

"Mine too."

♫

♫

Chapter Thirty-One

I wish, Beth thought as she dressed for her wedding, *I wish I could be like Joanna. Composed, calm, cool, competent.*

When she thought of Joanna, she thought of serenity, while she herself was turbulence. She was so excited that she had trouble pulling the pink silk dress over her head. She had a red spot on her forehead where she had burned herself with the curling iron. She couldn't find her lipstick.

As always, Ben waited patiently – waiting to take her to her wedding, waiting to take care of Benjie during her honeymoon, waiting to finish his doctoral studies, waiting to marry Joanna. Beth swallowed, and the air in her throat felt like a rock.

Her parents were not coming to the ceremony, but Ed's parents would be there. *Perhaps that's why I feel so jittery.* The strand of pale pink pearls was a wedding gift from Ed, and she could not make the catch work. "Ben, come fasten my pearls, please? My hands won't cooperate."

Ben came in and stopped short when he saw her. His eyes widened. "You're gorgeous, Sis!"

"I'm about as nervous as a burglar at a police convention."

He chuckled. "You'll do just fine – and, Beth, honey, you'll make a wonderful wife for Ed."

Impulsively she threw her arms around him. "I'll miss living with you, Ben."

"It'd be a little crowded – but I'll be around when you need me, no matter where I live."

Her eyes filled with tears. "I know, Big Brother, and I love you."

"If we don't go soon, you'll not become Mrs. Edward Westmoreland."

She giggled. "Say it again. The name. It sounds so – so . . . aristocratic."

Ben laughed. "Come on, Benjie, my boy. Let's go to your mama's wedding."

Beth knelt to straighten her son's tie, which matched Ed's.

"You'll be good and mind Ben while I'm gone, won't you, Benjie?"

"Benjie go fishing with Uncle Ben."

Beth stood up and said to her brother, "I know you'd rather be going on your own honeymoon. It's a long time before spring vacation. You'll use all your Christmas vacation taking care of Benjie."

"There's plenty of time for Joanna and me. Look, Sis! The first snowflakes!"

"Oh, Ben! I've always wanted to be married in the snow."

♬ ♬ ♬

I wish, Joanna thought as she dressed for the wedding, *I wish I could be like Beth. Vivacious, buoyant, natural, sparkling.*

Beth was unpolished, but she had an exuberance and resiliency that Joanna longed to emulate. She felt dull and colorless in comparison, and as old as Grandfather Mountain lately.

Well, Beth wasn't always this way, Joanna reminded herself as she thought about the lonely, sad girl who stumbled into her shop last August. She had seemed like a baby sparrow that Joanna wanted to cup in her hands and protect.

"My brother," she had said, explaining her relationship with Ben, and jump-starting the batteries to Joanna's heart. Going into the kitchen to check on the wedding cake, Joanna looked out the door, into the back yard and remembered a scene from her childhood when her faithful German shepherd spent the afternoon guarding a fledgling robin that had fallen from its nest. Cheyenne chased away the neighbor's cat and maintained her steadfast vigil until late afternoon, when Nicholas came home from work. He set up a stepladder and gently placed the bird back in its nest, much to the anxious mother's relief. They had watched the nest all summer until the three young robins were able to fly.

Joanna had spent the fall watching Beth. Ben had faithfully guarded her until Ed came into her life. *Perhaps now she's ready to fly.*

Ed had a youthfulness in his stride and voice since Beth came into his life. *Who would have thought Beth could bring such joy to Edward Westmoreland?*

Joanna put on her mother's diamond earrings and went to see if her father was ready.

♫ ♫ ♫

After Ben sang "A Wedding Prayer," he and Joanna moved to their places beside the bride and groom. Benjie positioned himself next to Nicholas's wheelchair, leaning against it, with the old gentleman's arm around him. Ed's parents and the few other guests waited expectantly for the ceremony to begin. Joanna had watched the look on the faces of Ed's parents. They were bursting with pride in their son and not at all overwhelmed with his new instant family.

Joanna was puzzled by Beth's bewildered face. She seemed disoriented. *What can be wrong?* Her pale countenance and the anxious expression in her eyes reminded Joanna of a neglected waif, an image Beth had not projected in months. *Is she regretting the marriage already?*

The minister began, "Dearly beloved, we are gathered here . . ."

Beth's face was chalk-colored, her lips blue. Joanna prepared herself, should it become necessary to assist her if she fainted. *I thought the groom was more likely to keel over at a wedding.*

"Do you, Edward, take this woman to be your lawful wedded wife? To have and to hold, to cherish . . . ?"

Ed, gazing down on his bride, almost flubbed his only line. Then, as though someone nudged him, he jerked up his chin and spoke in a firm, assured voice. "I *do*, sir."

Joanna saw a sudden change in Beth. Her eyebrows arched upward, and her cheeks blushed pink. Her sagging shoulders straightened, and a look of wonder radiated across her face. She raised her eyes to gaze at Ed. His resolute affirmation had infused her with confidence.

"Do you, Beth, take this man to be your lawful wedded husband? To have and – ?"

"Yes, sir, Preacher. I do!"

The minister, disconcerted, paused a fraction of a second, but no one snickered.

Ed beamed as the minister pronounced them husband and wife.

"You may kiss your bride."

That he did.

♫

♫

Chapter Thirty-Two

The lawn appeared buried under a white chenille bedspread, and snow was blowing across the doorstep when Joanna answered the door.

"Ben! Maybe we'll be snowbound and you'll have to spend the night with us."

"I'd like that." He folded her in his arms.

In Nicholas's room, Mrs. Campbell and Joanna had moved the bed so the patient could see the lighted Christmas tree in the yard.

"Why didn't you wait for me to move the bed?" Ben asked.

"He was impatient."

Joanna had set up a small tree on his dresser.

"Honeymooners back?" Nicholas asked.

"About an hour ago. Had a wonderful time. Both of them look as contented as my old Irish setter on a camping trip. They said they'll see you tomorrow." Ben's voice trembled with excitement. "I have something to show you two. You won't believe it."

"A marriage license?" Nicholas asked hopefully. "Wedding rings?"

Joanna spoke up. "Dad, you know I won't get married until you're better."

Nicholas patted her hand as she busied herself fluffing up his pillows, but he did not pursue the subject.

"What have you got, Ben?" he asked.

He pulled an envelope from his coat pocket and slowly withdrew a manila sheet, which he unfolded and dangled in front of them as if to tantalize them. Joanna saw an official-looking address embossed across the top.

"You read it, Nicholas," Ben said.

Nicholas perched his reading glasses on his nose, and his voice resonated as he read in a stilted theatrical voice.

"Dear Mr. Benensen . . . I am writing to inquire if you are still interested in the Oxford fellowship. Our current recipient is unable to complete his residency, and the position will be available beginning with the summer term."

Nicholas dropped the letter and slapped his hands together. Joanna squealed and leaped up to hug Ben.

"Told you!" Nicholas exclaimed. "I told you there would be a way."

"It's only for a year, Nicholas, and I need two."

"Look son. This is too good to lose. I'm not a rich man, but . . ."

Ben held up his hand. "No. Now listen. Joanna and I can work it out."

She faced her father. "I've reminded him that he found the manuscript. We'll share the profits – "

"Sounds right to me," Nicholas declared.

"Provided he uses it to go back to school," she said.

Ben wagged his head like an old dog and grinned. "Not even married, and she's telling me how to spend the money."

Nicholas's strength diminished rapidly. Ben took turns with Joanna at keeping watch beside his bed at night. Nicholas didn't want a night nurse, and Joanna was reluctant to leave him.

Andy and his family arrived on Christmas Eve.

Two nights later, Nicholas said softly, "I hear the angels singing. Do you hear the angels, Jo . . . ? Andy . . . ?"

♫ ♫ ♫

The house was so crowded that Joanna felt suffocated. "I'll be back," she told Ben and slipped away, rejecting his offer to accompany her.

She drove numbly through the sleeping community, following the streets randomly at first, winding through the little mountain village, ending up in the church parking lot. Using the penlight attached to her key ring to find her way, she stumbled to the church door. Inside, she turned on only the lights that were necessary to reach the organ.

She had always felt close to her mother there, and tonight she experienced her father's presence too.

Anesthetized by grief, she stood in front of the console. The music light gave only faint illumination in the cavernous building. The darkness folded around her like theater curtains, granting her an intimate privacy on the turf she knew best.

She kept her coat on and, with gloved hands, opened the instrument's lid. Craving only the quietness and solitude of the church, she made no effort to select music. She had yet to cry, but the aching in her heart was excruciating.

Scarcely aware of her actions, Joanna raised her right hand and caressed a key. The mute organ brought her to reality, and automatically she turned on the power. By habit she pulled out her favorite stop. Again she touched a key, and one lone, poignant note echoed in the church like a desolate wail.

She jerked her hand away from the instrument as though the key was red-hot.

Slowly she positioned her hand again and, with a gloved finger, traced the opening notes of a song she learned as a child. It carried her back to her youth . . .

♬

"He's got the whole world in His hands . . ."

♬

She had sat down on the piano bench after her mother had been practicing. With a straight little pointer she picked out the Negro spiritual, accompanying herself as she sang.

"Good, honey," her mother said. "Go on."

♬

"He's got the tiny little baby in His hands . . ."

♬

"Lovely, dear. Keep playing."

With a burst of conviction Joanna, not yet four, broke into joyful song, making up her own words.

♬

He's got the mommy and the daddy in His hands!
He's got the mommy and the daddy in His hands!

She played the spiritual now with her right hand only, a single note at a time, a plaintive lament in the chilled dark church. The notes reverberated from the rock walls, sustaining the flute-like tone and carrying the sound and her grief to the balcony. She bowed her head and closed her eyes.

"He's got you and me, brother, in His hands." She spoke the words aloud in a thin, sad voice as the tears flowed down her cheeks. "He's got you and me, Andy, in His hands . . ."

In the lonely stillness of the night, she yearned for comfort. She thought of the long talks she shared recently with her father.

She remembered his telling Ben, "Jo's mother thought she would compose masterpieces."

She had not thought of her earlier compositions in years. Looking at her hands, she was startled to see that she still wore her gloves. She pulled them off. The ivory keys were cold to her touch, and she shivered.

Joanna was about eight when her mother helped her record the notes to a short composition, "Falling Snowflakes."

How long has it been since I thought of that ditty?

She could not remember the words she had written, but she played the piece now, using only two chords, just as she wrote it. The simplicity of it, the childlike quality, seemed fitting to her now as Joanna sat alone in the sanctuary, vulnerable and grief-stricken.

She slipped off her loafers. The building was too frigid for her to buckle her organ shoes, but she slipped her feet into them. Hardly aware that she was doing it, she explored the maple pedals, ignoring the cold that cut through the thin soles. The narrow pedals hurt her feet, but the pain penetrated the veil of her anguish.

Her first significant organ arrangement had been an adaptation of "Jesus Loves Me," and she recalled it now. She adjusted the stops and played it as she arranged it in high school.

She repeated the composition, improvising, embellishing, adding stops, and increasing the crescendo. Quite unexpectedly she began to integrate phrases of the spiritual, "He's Got the Whole World in His Hands," weaving the two melodies in a harmonious musical tapestry. The childlike assurance of the hymn blended into the confidence of the lilting spiritual.

It was the first time in months that the creative muse had called to her.

"Dad," she said, her voice trembling, "I'll go back to work. I might not produce masterpieces, but I'll put my heart and soul into writing something you and Mother would be proud of."

The cascade of tears made it difficult to see the keys when she began to play Handel.

Nicholas had said, "Death is nothing to fear."

For her mother's funeral he requested "I Know That My Redeemer Liveth" from *Messiah*, and Joanna knew he wanted it played at his service. The words enunciated his faith, and tonight they inspired hers.

The organ responded to her touch, creating a duet with the timorous song in her heart. The rendition lacked the pulsing, tumultuous vigor of the "Hallelujah Chorus," but the voice of the organ sang of victory.

How long she played, Joanna did not know or care. She was sure Ben and Andy would guess where she was. Her fingers and feet felt frozen. She was near exhaustion, but still she lingered.

She was aware because of the hallway light that someone had opened the door, and although she could not hear his footsteps, she knew that Ben had joined her.

"Can you let him go yet?" he asked.

"At least they're together again." She leaned her head back against him and wept. "Ben, I want to be married at once."

He pulled her into his arms. "I know, sweetheart."

♫

♫

Chapter Thirty-Three

It was a William Wordsworth spring, with yellow banks of daffodils dancing in the breeze. The dogwoods wore bridal tiaras of white blossoms, a faint reminder of winter snows in the mountains.

They drove to Atlanta to be married quietly in Andy's home. Joanna chose an amethyst dress and added her mother's long white pearls. Betty and Andy gave her pearl earrings to match the necklace.

Andy put his arm around Joanna. "I've never seen you more beautiful. I wish Mother and Dad could see how happy you are."

"They know," Betty said.

Ben agreed.

"Aunt Joanna," her older niece Christy said, "you're more beautiful than a movie star."

Sarah added, "You should write a book on elegance, Aunt Joanna."

The honeymoon was short because of Ben's limited Easter break, but their homecoming was heralded with a gala reception hosted by the church choir. There were luncheons, dinners, and showers.

Joanna wondered when she would have time to prepare for their move to England.

For her wedding gift Ben gave her a folder of brochures on famous organs in Europe, including Westminster Abbey, London's St. Paul's, St. James, Piccadilly, and Christ Church in Oxford. Tucked in were letters of introduction to several renowned organists, directors of music, and university professors.

Joanna stared, amazed at the information. "How did you manage this?"

Ben cleared his throat, struggling to repress a smile. "I know a few people in high places."

She had saved the most interesting of Mr. Henry's books as a wedding gift. Ben opened the copy of Milton's *Paradise Lost*, and the look of awe on his face filled her with gratitude.

"When did you hide this?" he asked.

"Soon after we found the books. I thought it would be the ideal wedding gift for you."

She blushed, and he laughed. "You had your eye on me then?"

"Oh, leave me alone!"

He pulled her close to him and kissed away her embarrassment.

Beth and Ed would buy The Gilded Teapot and live in Joanna's home while building their own.

"How can everything fall into place so easily?" she asked Ben.

"Easily? Joanna Jerome Benenson, we have waited all our lives for this opportunity!"

"And each other."

"And each other."

♫ ♫ ♫

"Only one more stop," Joanna said as Ben picked up the last suitcase.

He nodded and led her to the car.

The small cemetery, tucked between high-rising summits, had roots before the Revolutionary War. A few tombstones dated back to the early 1700s; others marked the graves of Civil War veterans. The burial site offered a peaceful haven that looked as old as the surrounding mountains. The neatly kept lawn, changing from brown to spring green, spread across the crest and down the incline like a warm afghan. It was too early in the year for the scent of freshly mowed grass.

Joanna drank in the mountain fragrances of pine and fir. As she and Ben stood on the sun-drenched ridge, she noted that the more recent gravestones appeared bleached among the grayer lichen-etched ones. She bent to touch her mother's stone, then caressed her father's. The polished marble felt cool in the bright sunshine.

"I know lots of people, twice as old as I am, who still have both parents," she said. "I don't know why He took mine."

"Except that heaven is a far better plan than the best this world has to offer."

Ben examined her with dark eyes filled with tenderness and concern. He extended his hand to her, and when Joanna stood, he wrapped his arm around her. "Do you want to be alone for a few minutes," he asked, "for some time to remember?"

"Alone? Without you?" She shivered. "Without you is devastation."

He bit his lip and nodded.

They turned east and raised their eyes to the lofty granite peak of Grandfather Mountain. It stood like a majestic sentinel, guarding the old cemetery. To the right, beyond the mountain range, they would catch a plane from Charlotte to England in just a few short hours.

"I always felt sheltered by the mountains," Joanna murmured. "It's scary to leave."

"We'll come back. You've been away before."

"Yes . . . and I'm going with you. That's my safety."

He leaned down to kiss her gently. "Your Dad told us to trust in the Lord and He would give us the desires of our heart. And He has. We'll miss our plane, darling and the desire of my heart, if we don't go."

Ed, Beth, and Benjie were waiting for them at the parking lot, and as they descended the mountain, the child bounded toward them.

"Uncle Ben! Aunt Jo-annie! Benjie wanta go on airplane with you."

Ben scooped his nephew into his arms. "And leave your mother and Ed? What about your new puppy?"

"Take White Rags too."

Joanna kissed his cheek. "You need to help your daddy plan the new house, and we'll be back before you know it. Ed's bringing all of you to see us next summer."

Benjie cocked his head, and the pensive expression that filled his face was so much like Beth's that Joanna felt her heart constricting with sadness.

"I don't want to leave you, honey . . . or any of you!" She spread out her arms to enfold Beth and Ed. Beth clung to her for a few minutes.

"We all go," Benjie said.

"Right, son. We'll all go to the airport," Ed responded, glancing nervously at his watch. "It's going to be a close squeeze in the back seat for the three of you."

"I like that," Ben said.

"I'll sit back there, Ben." Beth said.

"Thanks, Sis, but I want to sit by my bride."

He lifted Benjie into his car seat and adjusted the straps.

"Go," Benjie shouted. "Go down the mountain!"

Ed eased the repaired BMW smoothly into gear. "Down the mountain."

"To England," Ben said.

Joanna heard his excitement, and she wriggled closer to him. She felt a stirring of emotion too, and a premonition that something extraordinary was happening. She had felt that same sense of expectancy once before, one morning last fall in her small tea room in Galax Falls, North Carolina.

Joanna sighed, smiled, and raised her face to look at her husband. "You said that day that I didn't care much for men."

He frowned. "When? Where? What day?"

"Never mind. I'll tell you later. I promise."

"Why does that line sound familiar, Mrs. Benenson?"

"Come to think of it, I believe I've heard it before, too."

Benjie leaned forward, turned in his car seat, and studied Joanna, a quizzical expression clouding his eyes momentarily. His face relaxed, reflecting the joy he saw in hers, and they laughed together.

"What's so funny?" Ben asked.

Benjie promised, "Tell you later, Uncle Ben."

♫ ♫

♫ ♫

♫ ♫